EXCERPT Magazine No. 2
Copyright ©2024
ISBN: 978-0-9855180-4-2
www.excerptmag.com

Editor's Note

Dear Reader,

You are about to embark on a journey into eight fictive dreams—novel excerpts from emerging writers with unpublished manuscripts or books recently/soon-to-be-published from small presses. You will travel from the mountains of North Carolina to India, New York, rehab alley in Delray. There will be summer camps and religious cults, grifter fathers and zombie brokers, and the mystery of a 19th-century naturalist and his voyages in search of a creature known as the yu-mau.

We are in a critical time for stories and storytelling. Maybe we always are. The existential threat of climate chaos. Book banning and censorship. The slow walk into neo-fascism, the tribalism of identity politics, the emergence of AI and the tech idiots who think it's a brilliant idea to feed the data beast our subconscious through art. Sometimes it feels like we're living in a bouncing castle at the end of the world.

To imagine in this day and age (instead of having your imagination fed 24/7) is a radical act. The simple act of opening a novel immerses you in the river of time and the messy humanity of others. Stories act as omens and collective dreams. Stories give us hope. Stories speak to the perpetual weaving of myths, cultures, histories. Stories open minds, challenge perceptions, and instigate paradigm shifts through connecting you, the anonymous reader, with something greater than yourself. Stories can't be muzzled, no matter how hard the religious zealots or tech nihilists may try. They pass as freely as the wind.

Keep reading, keep writing, keep imagining. Stay calm and *nolite te bastardes carborundorum.*

DW Ardern
Editor-in-Chief

EXCERPT MAGAZINE

No. 2   Spring 2024

In This Issue

Masthead

DW Ardern   Editor-in-Chief
Jenny Maattala   Fiction Editor
Cam Terwilliger   Fiction Editor
Isaac High   Assistant Editor
Justin Richel   Cover Artist

PAY ATTENTION, REMEMBER THIS

by

MARA AGUILAR EGAN

<u>Now</u>

A BIRD TRAPPED IN THE AIRPORT—something small and desperate and otherwise common, except for the distinction of being a frantic and wild thing amongst so many Jamba Juices.

He could hear the breathy flap of wing overhead as the thing swooped towards a wall of glass through which the sun rose into excruciating color. Sickening, the light of this dreaded day.

Sickening, the sound of beak cracking against glass.

No one else had noticed. If they had, they walked onward with only the briefest grimace—busy, late, aware that nothing could be done. Dennis was aware of this, too, but his mother was a woman who thought birds were omens—ignoring a suffering one could land you a curse.

But they were calling his zone.

Dennis liked this about airports, the disembodied voice telling him what to do was the closest he got anymore to believing in a higher power. As he crammed into 23B, Dennis added the bird to a running list in his head—a tally of the day's miseries. He wanted to believe that an army of little shitty things became more than the sum of their parts and hoped that by consolidating and ordering his dull unhappiness, he might redeem it—a collector of mundane suffering, he considered himself, the Patron Saint of Stubbed Toes. So far, he had:

> ~ *airport bird*
> ~ *airport mothers yelling at airport children*
> ~ *the possibility of seeing the people who* ~~used to love~~ *probably hate you*
> ~ *jaw ache so bad you fantasize about sawing off the bottom half of your face*
> ~ *at least everyone would feel sorry for you coming back with half a face like that*
> ~ *the fact you had this thought ^ before listing…*
> ~ *your mother is in open-heart surgery*
> ~ *she's expecting you*

Like misery, Dennis thought of his mother in fragments—the way she walked with her hands curled in loose fists; the panic in her voice when she said, *wait*, stopped and dug through a purse full of receipts and melting lipsticks and nickels covered in dog-haired grime (they'd never had a dog), searching for keys. There was the sudden appearance of her pale tongue as she licked drips of chocolate-ice-cream-for-dinner from her hand, her brow furrowing like she'd forgotten that ice cream could melt. The way her wrists would glisten—the alchemy of saliva and sugar leaving slug trails over her thin skin. Such thin skin.

It was an unfair and bizarre rule of this world, Dennis thought as the plane lifted, that the bird, longing for open air and origin, was stuck in the airport, and that Dennis, with no desire to return home, was on his way.

Dennis had given himself one week to make things right with his mother, with the people he hadn't seen or spoken to since his last time home—the most remarkable and terrible night of his unremarkable life, with the nagging voice he heard when he tried to sleep, whispering, *coward, coward, you piece of shit.*

*

Hours later, as he drove his rental car through western North Carolina, he found himself thinking of the bird's bones. The closer he got to his hometown, his own felt so insubstantial, he wondered if they too might be hollow. It was a feeling of overinflation, as if the place whirring past his window was instead inside his chest—blue mountain air tightening his lungs, poison sumac cracking between his ribs.

The ecosystem inside his body had been dormant since he'd been away, nine whole years of inner winter. Now it was stirring—a bear blinking out of hibernation, a snake finished with old skin.

He added one more bullet to his mental list:

~ *being trapped inside your own melodramatic mind*

His worrying mind, Dennis was convinced, was what kept the world spinning. He knew he should be worrying about the warming planet, about all the people and all the birds his mother said were dying because of it, but mostly, he worried about his mother dying. His saving grace was that he'd learned there is protective magic in anticipating things— it's the bad things you've never even considered that happen.

So he made himself imagine every scenario, *see it,* lie awake at night going through a list of ways he might lose her:

~ *car accident*
~ *mass shooting*
~ *heart attack*
~ *murder/suicide*
~ *regular murder*
~ *regular suicide*

He'd imagined her death so many times growing up, but never the way she was dying now, so ordinary. In a thin bed at the very hospital where she'd worked as a CNA.

He was so sure someone would kill her, one of the boyfriends she'd fight with while Dennis huddled in his room with headphones on, staring at the blue light from the portable CD player that seemed to have the power to stare back. Dennis remembered begging that blue light not to let the music skip. The disc inside, a mix of his mother's, was covered in scratches faint as old scars. When his magic failed and the music stuttered, Dennis could hear the specifics of his mother's fights with men whose names Dennis would forget more easily than the timbre of their voices when the words, *you stupid fucking cunt,* slipped through a crack in Van Morrison's "Days Like This."

The fight was particularly bad on the night that CD finally stopped playing. Dennis left his room, tiptoeing down the short, dark hall. At the edge of it, he got low, his knees and palms pressing into the itchy carpet so that, when he peered around the corner, the half moon of his face wouldn't catch their eye.

He could see the boyfriend's back, his mother's face. His stomach clenched at her expression—the twist of her mouth, vibration of her eyes inside her skull. She was still in her scrubs. Splattered blood would just look like a day's work.

The boyfriend stepped towards her over shards of a favorite vase—an orange and turquoise thing that had belonged to his mother's mother, who they did not discuss. A book lay open on the ground beneath them, and Dennis wondered which had been thrown first and by whom. His mother's favorite poem was in that book, one he'd memorized for her as a Christmas present. She'd cried when he'd recited it for her, so it had either made her very happy or very sad. The line, *it cannot hurt me when I'm old,* still got stuck in his head.

"You think you can kick me out?" the boyfriend said. "Who bought the food in your fridge, Naomi? The booze in your cabinet?"

"Take it," she said. "Take your shitty food and your

shitty booze and never bring your succubus energy in my house again."

"My *suck-you-what* energy? Look at you," he said. "Look at you and your shithole house and your retard kid."

Dennis didn't even think to be insulted, he was too surprised to hear himself exist in this adult exchange. But his mother's anger took root in something quieter, more dangerous.

"Get out," she said. Now it was she who Dennis worried might do the killing. She stepped closer. She did not even seem to feel the piece of porcelain that sliced into the sole of her slender bare foot. "Get out of my house."

Dennis watched the man's back rise and fall, waiting for him to strike her, wondering if he would be brave enough to try to stop him. Instead, the man turned and stalked away.

"You," he said, "are a hopeless woman."

Despite her pitbull stance, his mother flinched at the slamming of the door. Dennis flinched at her flinch, and the movement must have caught her eye. She looked right at him, "Did you hear?"

Of course he'd heard. Even if he hadn't snuck out of his room, their rental was the size of a TV family's kitchen.

"Do you know what it means?"

He stood, brushing off his stinging knees, nodded.

"Then you know it isn't true, yes? What he said about you."

Dennis bit down on his chapped lip, pulled on a shred of skin still attached enough to hurt. Yes, he knew it wasn't true, but it was evidence of how not normal Dennis was that the man had even thought to say it.

"It would help if you talked more," she said. "Stared less."

Dennis shrugged.

That made her laugh. "Bring me the bottles on the counter, Charlie Chaplin."

Dennis didn't know who Charlie was, but he went for the bottles anyway, one tall and full of brown liquid, the other short, orange plastic, like a little round traffic cone that warned of a dangerous route. These bottles had gone away for a while. They'd come back with the boyfriend. Dennis was careful not to step on any piece of the broken vase as he brought them to her. She had collapsed on the couch. Her face was no longer fearsome, but so slack and wet that Dennis wanted to grab fistfuls of her cheeks and lift them, stretch them upward until she either smiled or swallowed her own head.

"Do you love me?" She asked in a small, small voice.

Another nod.

She pulled him into her. Dennis pressed his face against her hot, soft neck, inhaling the mother scent of her, something meaty he associated with his own birth—like blood and shit and sharp first breath. Her arm maneuvered around him to either hold him or twist the cap of the little bottle. Both.

"You don't know yet, Dennis," she began, all the strength drained from her voice. "What it's like to wish for a different version of your life, of yourself, so badly you can feel it living inside your stomach." She shook two white circles into her palm and took a pull from the other bottle that he felt dribble on his head, the smell like either syrup or carpet cleaner.

"Like you swallowed a magnet," she went on, "that will rip through your middle trying to reach its match?"

Her voice was pleading.

"I know," Dennis said, even though he knew he couldn't understand. But also maybe he did. He felt like maybe he did. His mother returned the caps to both bottles and rested her cheek on the top of his head.

"But I have you."

This was not a comfort, he thought. This was a spell, a binding, a disappointment.

"I love you so much, you know that?"

"I know," he whispered into her neck, now moist with her tears and his own trapped breath.

"I love you so much it hurts, baby."

Saying this, she plunged the knife edge of her own hand into the folds of her belly, pushing hard against the flesh there. Digging, Dennis supposed, for the magnet she'd swallowed.

*

He'd woken at 3am the morning he flew from LAX to the Asheville Regional Airport. Forty minutes in a taxi, six hours on a plane, and twenty-six minutes in his rental car, and Dennis still wasn't ready. Not to be here, where the melting sun made every glint of window look like a memory and every passing driver look like someone he used to know. Not ready to see her.

Dennis, upon reaching his left turn, the one that would take him past the old rental, through downtown, and toward the hospital where his mother was waiting, turned right.

It was barely a decision that landed him on the Blue Ridge Parkway. A mere twitch of muscle memory that had him hugging curve after hypnotizing curve of the road's ascent toward the gaping mouth of the place in this world he once knew best, the summer camp where his mother had dropped him off seventeen years earlier.

There, smaller now. Camp Pinecrest, est. 1930. The entrance where he'd walked alone on that day he'd first met Fatima, Pete, and Tuck. It was little more than a gravel road, a gate, a vinyl banner, reading *Welcome Home*. Dennis could not see the camp from here, but he could feel it like a phantom limb or love at first sight, on which Dennis had mixed feelings but had reason to believe was something like swallowing an entire bottle of alka-seltzer or a magnet.

Through the crayon-scented heat of the still running car, Dennis felt the gravity of the things he could not help but remember: the lake, the creek bed, the house. The Bell House, that Southern Living monstrosity where four generations of camp directors—always Bells—had lived, pruning flame azaleas and laughing on a porch that wrapped around the house like a mother cradling her child.

That first summer, both Dennis and Tuck's mothers had been late to pick them up at the end of the session, so they'd been invited inside to Bell Family Dinner.

It had occurred to Dennis then that he'd never eaten

dinner at a table. The act of placing his cloth napkin in his lap as foreign to him as the Bell's salt—not the damp cardboard container of Morton's above the microwave, but large, fat flakes kept in a wooden bowl at the table's heart.

After grace, Mrs. Bell lifted her glass of butter-colored wine, "To the best summer yet."

Coach shook his head, a muscle jumping in his superhero jaw. "Two instances of anaphylactic shock. Down with yellow jackets, I say. Down with peanut butter."

"Dad's never happy with camp," Pete explained to the other boys, adding more parmesan to his spaghetti. Tuck held his fork in a fist like a toddler.

"My husband can't be proud of something unless it's absolutely perfect."

Pete, almost imperceptibly, flinched.

"He's obsessive," Mrs. Bell added with a tinge of pride, as if her husband's perfectionism reflected favorably on his choice of wife, which, watching her take a small sip of wine, Dennis supposed it did. Even her swallow was lovely— a measured invitation.

"Why shouldn't I be?" Coach asked. "What are we working for if it's not going to be extraordinary? What do I mean then?"

Dennis paused mid-bite, a saucy onion slipping from a noodle to his lap. He had never heard an adult, or anyone, speak like this. He had never been asked such a big question.

"I don't know, Love." Mrs. Bell dabbed at her mouth. "What *do* you mean?"

The light from their antler chandelier caught in Coach's eyes like magic, like possession. "I'm serious," he said. "What is the point if it's not exquisite? Why waste our time?"

The boys sat still and small, feeling the absence of Fatima, the girl who always knew what to say. Whose mother was on time. Who would be halfway back to Florida by now. Then Tuck's hand shot up. It was always the most erect part of that round boy, his raised hand.

"You don't have to raise your hand at the dinner table, Tuck," Mrs. Bell said.

"Sorry. But you make things as good as you can. Everything you do," he said. "For the glory of God."

Coach made a throat noise that sounded appreciative, if not convinced. He looked to his son.

"You asking me?" Pete said.

"I'm asking the future assistant director of Camp Pinecrest."

"You mean, like, what's the point of camp?"

The man leaned in, ashen elbows sliding back as he gripped the tablecloth and brought himself as close to the boys as he could without leaving his seat. "What's the point of being human if not to make something like that?" he asked. "What's the point of being alive?"

Dennis couldn't let a question go unanswered. When Pete didn't speak and Tuck didn't come to his rescue, he clenched his fists and made himself answer.

"Maybe just to be alive," he said. "Maybe the point of being alive is just that, to be really alive."

It was the flustered answer of a twelve-year-old boy, but Coach turned to Dennis, focused all of his Coachness right at him like a beam of tangible heat, and smiled.

"And what does it mean to be really alive?"

You tell me, Dennis thought. Please. Please, tell me.

It was an accident Dennis was at this table, another consequence of his mother's chronic lateness, but he felt, even then, like he was entering a conversation that would last the rest of his life. He stared at the candlelight between Coach and Mrs. Bell, the wicks left too long so that the flame flickered erratically, simultaneously threatening to extinguish or catch fire to everything.

Dennis imagined the heat of it all—the flame, Coach's question, his own burning desire to remain in this circle of golden people—melting off his lips, his cheeks, then every inch of him. The pale candle of himself dripping off his embarrassing boyskin. It would ooze away from him and slither to the bottom of that shining lake at the center of camp, and he would be left pink and soft and nothing and good.

It would be seven summers after that first dinner that two of the people sitting at the table really would melt. From the inside out, choking on nothing but moonlight and their own failing livers. Their skin would turn as yellow as the wine in Mrs. Bell's glass as they grew unbearably sleepy under a Silver Oak. It would be like an echo of a story people around these parts liked to tell, a warning to children about wasting time.

Are you standing in the river? Coach would ask the boys

if he came across one of them on the grounds, eyes closed to a breeze or squinting up at the night sky. *Are you standing in the river right now?*

Dennis never understood that question. He was not standing in a river, but on the same gravel road that led up to that house. It crunched beneath him, the sound familiar and hungry like the growl of his own belly. He didn't remember parking the car or stepping into the air, heavier here than it was in California—thick and tired. He patted his shirt pocket, making sure the car key was there. Though he felt the shape of it against his chest, he could not shake the feeling that there was something he'd lost as he peered up at the torn and mildewed banner.

"Welcome home," he said to himself.

THEN

DENNIS HAD LOST any excitement he'd had for summer camp—it tumbled off the roof of his mom's car along with a donut and an iced coffee, all of it smacking the tar like a heart attack, the cream already curdling in the high summer sun.

She had overslept, taken twenty-seven minutes to find her keys, and then missed her turn, so they were inevitably running late to the first inevitably terrible day of what Dennis assumed would be his first—and last—inevitably terrible summer at Camp Pinecrest.

She screeched to a halt, cursing as the yellow light turned red.

The streetlight's swinging red eye stared at Dennis, the unblinking glow reminding him of how they'd ended up here.

The morning after his mother told him about the magnets in her belly, he'd awoken to the muffled sound of Joni Mitchell's "Circle Game." He'd followed the sound to the living room where the mess from the night before was all but erased. Instead of the bottles, on the kitchen counter sat a ripped open envelope addressed to his mother in looping cursive. Dennis had been curious about it when it arrived weeks earlier: a real letter! But his mother had buried it beneath the water bills and glossy junk addressed to all the strangers who had lived here before. He had thought he'd seen her hand shake, but sometimes they did that when she was in pain or in love or too tired or too awake.

He found her sitting just beyond the pollen-coated slab of concrete they called the front porch, the screen door whining behind him as he stepped out.

She was nested in the plot of dirt, surrounded by plants that were wilted and half unearthed, like they'd tried crawling to friendlier soil. His mother had brought home the small, flowering plants with Wal-Mart Garden Center clearance tags after one of the many fights with her boyfriend. She'd said they were going to have a garden. She'd said they would be able to pick their own flowers, put them in the vase, and have lilies on the table like fancy people, but she'd be too tired to water them for weeks at a time and then in a moment of energy and desperation, soak them. Both, Dennis had heard, were bad for growing things.

His mother was watching him closely. "We don't need these kinds of flowers," she said. "The honeysuckle grows for free out back."

"Coffee?" She offered him one of the two mugs beside her. He took the pale one, a cup of milk and sugar into which his mother would periodically splash some of her real stuff, turning a pleasing beige. It was a ritual for mornings when it was just the two of them in the house.

As he sat beside her, he realized that the air felt good, a clean bite, the relief of early fall.

"Listen to this, Den," she read, flipping a page of one of the magazines she'd stolen from the hospital waiting rooms. "In the 19th century, nostalgia was considered a disease among soldiers. The Swiss were so likely to become nostalgic listening to this one song that playing it became *punishable by death.* The Russians buried nostalgic soldiers alive. But the Americans…" she put up air quotes with her coffee-holding hand and didn't flinch when the brown liquid spilled over, splattering on the dust beneath her, "…considered men who suffered from nostalgia weak-minded and idle. They treated the disease with demonstrations of public humiliation and shaming." She scoffed. "Can you imagine, Den, being buried alive just for listening to a song?"

She lifted both arms into the crisp sky, coffee tilting again at a dangerous angle. There was an edge to her this morning—something quivering beneath the surface of her. She sucked a deep breath through her nose as she wiggled her fingers, waving at the leaves the color of orange juice that whirled down around them. "Being buried alive just for missing autumn?"

Dennis laughed—small and strangled—at the image of them both buried under leaves, all those colors, bursting upwards like ladies from a cake in an old movie.

Dennis' mother answered his laugh with her own shy smile and pulled another magazine from behind the first. Not a magazine, Dennis saw, but a brochure. On the cover, a girl with French braids smiling big with the kind of buck teeth that make adults love you. Her tie-dyed t-shirt read, *Camp*

Pinecrest Est. 1930.

"How would you like to go to summer camp this year?"

Dennis scrunched his nose. The only notion he had of such things had to do with Freddy Krueger and horse girls, neither of which he wanted anything to do with. "We can't afford summer camp," he said.

His mother blinked, surprised, maybe a touch angry, but quickly shook her head. "You don't have to worry about that."

Not worry? Dennis' mother was always worrying about things they couldn't afford or control—things like rising rent and a hole in the sky. He wondered if she worried about that hole in the sky to keep it from growing.

"God, you're so serious," his mother said as if noticing this for the first time. "Look, you don't have to worry because you got a scholarship."

This only confused Dennis more. "Why?"

"Because," his mother gripped his chin, made him look into her volcano eyes. "You're very, very smart. And smart kids get scholarships."

Dennis stared at her face, the thin, purplish skin under her eyes, the wrinkles in the corners of her mouth, crusted with remnants of instant coffee. There was a sound like rain around them then, a descent of whirligigs.

His mother pulled her gaze from her son to watch.

"Snow!" she said. "In fall!"

Dennis knew one more magic trick—he could slow down time. He did this most often with the ceiling fan above his bed, focusing on one blade to follow it in circles until the spin was no longer a blur but something steady and trace-able. Now, in the flurry of seeds, he found a single whirligig to watch as it twirled, unhurriedly to the earth, his mother still beside him.

"Okay," he said when time didn't stop. "I'll go."

*

Summer had been a lifetime away in October. Dennis never thought it'd actually arrive until his mother pulled over outside the entrance to Camp Pinecrest.

"You can't drive me in?" he asked.

His mother wrinkled her nose, but didn't look at him. "I have a shift. I don't want to get stuck behind all those hover-mothers and jesus-jukers."

"What's a jesus-juker?"

"You're about to find out." She reached over him and opened his door.

"Here," she handed him a wad of fabric. "Your old ones are probably too small now."

Dennis fingered the Belk's clearance tags still dangling from the blue swimming trunks. Everything she bought him was blue. She thought it was his favorite color, but Dennis didn't have a favorite color. He thought, *what's your favorite color* was the stupidest, most half-assed question adults asked kids, and he refused to make up an answer just to have one.

"Thanks."

"Good luck," she said, and then, like it would pain her

to remain another second, she sped off, leaving Dennis under a banner welcoming him to a home he didn't know how to enter.

He took small steps, a thin pillow tucked under his arm, his mother's rolling suitcase dragging on the gravel road, as nervous and out of place as its young handler.

The first sign of life he came across was an unmanned folding table marked, *Registration.* There were clipboards and wristbands in traffic light colors, but no humans.

He panicked. This was all a sham, his mother had tricked and abandoned him. His breath became tight and shallow.

In: one, two, three. He had been taught a breathing technique by the school counselor the day he'd wet his pants in the afterschool pick-up line. She hadn't wrinkled her nose at him or told him he was too old for this. She'd only counted while he breathed.

He had waited for his mother for more than two hours, refusing to go to the bathroom in case he missed her. He remembered the sounds of cars passing like ocean waves— *closer, further, closer, further*—none of them slowing, none of them her.

Hold: one, two, three. When she'd showed up, she was unharmed. Had only lost track of time. Had only forgotten.

Out: one, two, three, four. It was important, the counselor had told him, to breathe out just a count longer than he breathed in. To empty himself before he filled up again.

As his chest loosened, he thought he could hear those

cars again, but it was more than that—a chorus of shouts and whistles and splashes.

Dennis followed the sound to a lake. Here were the people. The water was sprinkled with sunlight and kids in taffy-colored bathing suits, teenagers blowing whistles that hung from cords around their necks. The deet-laden summer air carried the mist of someone else's splash to Dennis' peach fuzz cheeks. It smelled like rotting leaves and sunshine.

Standing at the edge of the dock, a girl in a yellow one-piece bounced from foot to foot. She was shining and poofy-haired, and he could tell by the exaggerated way she geared up for her cannonball she had her fingers on the pulse of fun.

To Dennis' shock, her brown eyes looked right at him. He froze, excruciatingly aware of his hands, one sweating palm on the handle of his suitcase, the other limp at his side.

Her smile widened wider than her small face could handle, and she threw a peace sign.

When she leapt into the sunlit lake, everything stilled. Then exploded.

"That was a big splash," was the first thing Dennis Holloway ever said to Fatima Williams. White teeth, fruit punch breath, sun-swallowing face.

"Right?" she said. "I'm Fatima."

It was the most exotic name Dennis had ever heard. He wondered if he'd ever talked to such a dark girl before, then he mentally apologized for thinking that. Was he allowed to think that? There were groups of them at his school, but none of them had green eyes like this, and they made fun of his bird chest. The white girls did, too, but they were quieter about it, meaner but easier to pretend he didn't hear.

"Who are you?"

"My name's Dennis."

"Very nice to meet you, Dennis." Her handshake was oaken and sure. "I bet this is your first summer, huh?"

He could already feel it, how he would lose this girl. She would become an almost friend, bailing just as soon as she saw how weird he was—uninteresting, uncool, sticky.

"Well, yeah. At this camp," he lied. "I've gone to others before though."

"Yeah?" she raised her eyebrows, sensing but not seeming to mind the dishonesty. Dennis felt his cheeks heat and wanted to shrink.

"Kid, I've been here for only two hours," she went on, "and I already know that no one brings a rolling suitcase to summer camp. It's cool. It's my first summer, too. I'm just as nervous as you."

"Yeah?" It was his turn to raise his brows. She laughed. It was such a happy, liquid sound, Dennis wanted to drink it.

"Okay, no. I mean it is my first summer. But I can't be nervous. I'm too freaking excited."

"Excited…" Dennis tried on the word.

"For sure. I'm gonna perfect my cannonball and learn to canoe and sing in the talent show. Just wait until you hear me sing, Denny. I'm going to be a for real famous singer. Not like just how all kids think they're gonna be singers or actresses or, like, veterinarians. I have groove, my dude. Like, real groove. Like Whitney. That's what my mom says. She thinks Whitney has an artist's soul, though dad just thinks she's a popstar. Mom says he doesn't get it because he's white. But that's like a whole other thing." She waved her hand as if to say, we have time for that later. "What's most important is that you and I are gonna make the best friends of our whole lives this summer. My dad says so. He went here, you know."

Already, five minutes into knowing Fatima, his stomach roller-coastered at the notion of *you and I.* Already, she was the most exciting thing he'd ever been a part of. She had a nickname for him. She had a plan.

A holler trumpeted from the other side of the dock from where Fatima and Dennis stood as someone back-flipped off the slanted roof into the lake. A lifeguard blew a long *toooooot* and ran to the kid climbing out of the water, grinning. When he arrived at the end of the dock, his face softened like *oh you!* He put the boy in a headlock-noogie combo.

Fatima and Dennis watched the back-flipper dry off, water flicking from his dark blond hair as he shook his head like a golden retriever, pleased with himself and everything else.

Fatima grabbed Dennis' arm and squeezed, her hand the temperature of lakewater. "We'll have to be friends with him."

Dennis felt a nag somewhere deep in the center of his brain that being close to such an evident winner would mean he would always be losing. But watching the boy push his hair back, tan skin stretching over straight shoulders, he couldn't help wanting to be close.

"First though," Fatima said, letting her hand fall back to her hip, "tell me about yourself, Denny. Oh, I have a good first question: if you could be a lake, the ocean, a river, or rain, which would you choose and why?"

It was better than *what's your favorite color.*

Within a half hour, Fatima knew about Dennis' mother— her love of old music, poetry, and having ice cream for dinner, as well as her tiredness, and the startling fact that she didn't have a husband, that Dennis didn't have a dad.

She learned that his superpower would be *um, flying, I guess,* and he learned that hers would be the ability to draw any food and have it become real.

"That way you can eat whatever you want and no one would be hungry and also animals wouldn't have to die for burgers. Because I love cows. But I also love burgers. The drawing part, rather than just, like, snapping my fingers is so I have to develop a skill to harness my superpower. I don't want it making me lazy, you know."

She learned that Dennis would be the ocean if only because he couldn't wrap his head around the ocean and very much wanted to.

To that, she said, "Yeah, right? Like giant squids? Crazy."

Dennis laughed, and Fatima cocked her head at him. "I've never seen a smile like that. It's crooked. Like only half of your face is happy."

Dennis felt a flush spread up his cheeks and into his dark, flat hair.

"I like it," she decided.

THE SECOND VOYAGE
OF
AUDLEY WORTHINGTON

by

CHRISSY KOLAYA

Much of the island's interior is covered with dense jungle forests which our native guides describe as nearly impenetrable, though stories persist that the interior harbors a strange creature the natives call the yu-mau.

—Excerpt from the travel journals of Audley Worthington, courtesy of the Worthington Archives

The yu-mau is like a human, but not a human as we are.

—Belief among the Tardo people of Clove Island

The disappearance of Audley Worthington and the question of whether the yu-mau actually existed is one of the most enduring mysteries of our time. So you can understand the splash the news of the fossil discovery caused. This was no obscure branch of the human family tree, but the anthropological equivalent to finding out what became of Amelia Earhart.

—Dr. Maxine Wharton, conference proceedings, American Anthropological Association Annual Meeting

Mysteries appeal to us because they lack answers, not despite this.

—Adam Benedict

FOREWORD
BY DR. MAXINE WHARTON

If you are like most people, you'll want to know how I became interested in the disappearance of Audley Worthington.

I could tell you what I have told others—what has always seemed obvious to me: How could one not be drawn to such a mystery?

If you are like most people, you'll want to know: What happened to him?

You will want to know what I make of the discoveries: a belt buckle—might it be his? A Kater's Prismatic compass—at one time, it had perhaps borne an engraving, but now, worn and scratched, unreadable. Impossible to know.

You will want to know what I make of the yu-mau: indigenous folk tale? An actual creature—some hominid living alongside modern humans? And what of the fossil discovery?

How disappointing, though, to find everyone—always—asking the wrong questions.

First Voyage, 1870

Audley Worthington, newly twenty, steadied himself against the strange sensation of the ship rocking on the small waves that swelled among the docks, a motion that had already begun to unsettle his stomach. This, he worried, did not bode well for his fitness at sea. The ship's side—was it leeward? starboard?—bumped against the dock as Worthington concentrated on keeping his balance, his feet planted in a wide stance he hoped appeared natural. Did he imagine it, or were the sailors scowling at him?

He wondered whether the captain and crew knew his appointment as ship's naturalist had been secured through neither experience nor fitness for the expedition ahead, but rather thanks to the efforts of his uncle, Sir Owen Maynard. He hoped they did not.

Captain Roderick Fitzhugh stepped onto the deck, cleared his throat, then addressed the men assembled before him. From the port at Plymouth they would proceed first to Madeira for verification of their chronometers, from there to the Cape of Good Hope for a supply of water and to revictual and refit as necessary. Having done so, they would then make their way to Clove Island and its lone port at

Sampat on the southeastern side of the island. The goal of their voyage as laid out by the Admiralty was to survey the circumference of Clove Island in hopes of securing a location for the construction of a second port on the northernmost part of the island.

Worthington felt a swell lift, then lower the boat. He reached out for the deck's railing to steady himself. Around him, the water slapped against the side of the ship, hulls of smaller boats thumped against the docks, and wind set flapping a loose corner of sail. About the captain, he knew little.

"Fond of his drink, but reliable" had been his Uncle Maynard's terse summary of the character of the man who now stood before them, speaking.

Since securing his position, all of Worthington's worries had circled around the same concern: Would he prove himself worthy of his position as ship's naturalist, of his uncle Maynard's imprimatur? Or, would he instead bring shame upon the family name? There were so many opportunities— they seemed almost endless, really—by which he might fail to live up to his uncle's expectations. Unfitness for sea travel and adventure, lax collection and labelling methods, insufficient attention to the many tasks that fell to a ship's naturalist: recording meteorological conditions, conducting a geological survey, collecting samples of the flora and fauna, and making notes on the peoples of the island, their cultures and customs.

Uncle Maynard, himself a member of the Royal Society and a noted expert on mosses, had made it clear that he had every expectation Worthington would distinguish himself by way of this opportunity. At the send-off dinner his uncle had hosted the night before, he had lifted his glass and toasted Worthington: "To your good health, good fortune, and the making of a man."

That evening, after the guests departed, Maynard had led Worthington into Halham Hall's great library and gifted him a Kater's prismatic compass, his initials engraved on the back. He ran his fingers over it now, in his pocket, as he listened to the captain—the smooth outer case, the rough pattern of the engraved letters.

"In circumnavigating the island," the captain continued, "an accurate survey must be made showing Clove Island's anchorages and watering places, as well as the nature of the soil, and the kind of timber, along with a full investigation of the tides." Along the way, the captain explained, they would send accounts of their proceedings, state, and condition to the Admiralty.

Worthington had hoped he might find his shipmates companionable, but his early interactions had done little to encourage him, the sailors brusque and unfriendly as he loaded his things aboard, brushing past him, "look now!" in the tight corridor belowdecks. Now, he worried what it would be like—months with these men, out on the open sea—for even longer upon the island.

At least the expedition's artist, with whom he would be sharing a cabin, had seemed a good man. Worthington had not expected to be sharing quarters. He had imagined his cabin as a private refuge. But when he'd opened the door, he'd found a young man, tall and lean, stretched out on one of the bunks. The man leapt to his feet, smiling and offering his hand.

"Grenville," he'd said. "You must be Worthington."

Together, they had arranged the tiny cabin, settling on places to store Grenville's paints, sketchbooks, pencils, and easels, Worthington's swoop nets, bottles of preserving spirits, and the Wardian terrariums by which he might safely transport the island's botanical treasures. Worthington hoped the captain had seen fit to set aside ample storage space for the specimens he'd collect. Somewhere neither too dark, nor too damp. He'd read countless tales of specimens destroyed by careless preparation and storage.

Already the cabin was an overstuffed, chaotic jumble, but Grenville had seemed warm and friendly.

"May I?" Worthington had asked, pointing to the many sketchbooks spread out over Grenville's bunk.

"Certainly," Grenville said as he sorted through a collection of paintbrushes.

The sketchbook was only halfway used, the end papers still blank, as Worthington leafed through them. The opening pages, however, were filled with sketches, studies of what appeared to be the same beautiful young woman again and again, at different angles, with different expressions upon her face. Grenville's talent was plain. The man had clearly earned his position.

"What brought you to sign on for the voyage?" Worthington asked.

Grenville placed his paintbrushes back in the trunk, which sat open at the foot of his bed. "I have always dreamed of traveling," he said, "of seeing the world. So, when the opportunity arose by which I might do so while also making myself presentable as a candidate for marriage, I was as eager as a man can be."

"And you have someone in mind?"

"Miss Amelia Bates." Grenville's eyes glittered. He seemed to be picturing her, wherever she might be, rather than the crowded cabin around them.

"You must tell me all about her," Worthington said, closing the sketchbook.

"She is a pianist," Grenville began. "A true talent, with a warm heart and a gentle, kind disposition. Her family, however, is not eager to see her married to a penniless artist. With the salary I will earn as expedition artist, well, I hope they shall see their way to changing their minds upon my return. And what about you? Have you a young lady awaiting your return?"

"I'm afraid not. My mother, however, is quite intent on remedying that situation." Worthington smiled. "She tells me I am too focused on the work of natural science. I feel certain that by the time I return, she will have someone in mind."

"And what shall you do, after you return, aside from being married off by your mother?" Grenville asked.

Worthington thought for a moment. "I suppose I shall craft my notes from the voyage into a book on the natural history of the island."

"Well then," Grenville said, raising in his hand an imaginary glass with which to toast. "To men of art and science. A far more noble endeavor than these men of commerce and industry." As he said it, he gestured beyond the room, toward the rest of the ship—shouts from the deck and beyond, commotion in the corridor as the rest of the ship's men secured their own belongings and argued over bunks.

They'd been interrupted then, by shouts calling all men to the deck for the captain's address.

Worthington felt the breeze ruffle his hair, and on it came the fishy, salty smell of the docks. Overhead, birds called to each other, sharing some important news of the day as the captain continued: "A naturalist having been permitted to accompany you—" here, the captain gestured stiffly toward Worthington, who raised his hand in acknowledgment "—every reasonable facility is to be given him in making and preserving his collections." The members of the crew appeared entirely uninterested.

His quarry was meant to be a full and complete picture of the flora and fauna of the island, including expected and unexpected variations—differences in size, coloration, distinctions between the male and female of the species, between the juvenile and the adult. As a child, Worthington had been an avid collector of insects, much to the dismay of his mother, who had grown weary of finding, scattered around their home, the desiccated corpses of beetles affixed to paper, accompanied by Worthington's notes about their characteristics and the circumstances of their discovery.

Eventually, these early attempts had grown into a more systematic method of preserving and recording his specimens—local plants, dried and pressed into his journal, and the occasional animal bones and fossils, all of which he shared proudly with his Uncle Maynard when they visited.

His Uncle Maynard had praised these amateur collections, had invited Worthington, on each visit, into the great library at Halham Hall, where he carefully removed his own trays of specimens from the drawers he'd had built for them, and for hours they stood together, bent over these collections—beetles and butterflies, pressed flowers and delicate seed pods, Maynard pointing out some subtle difference between one variety and another. It was here that Worthington learned the principles of classification and care of his specimens, how to properly label and organize his own collections, how to carefully pin a specimen without damaging it. And it was here, in the great library at Halham Hall, that he had begun to itch for the world beyond the English countryside. When Worthington's father had died, Maynard, having no son of his own, had taken the boy under his wing, attending with great interest to his education and opportunities. Worthington read Pliny the Elder, Diodorus Siculus, Marco Polo's *Book of the Marvels of the World* in his uncle's library, wondering at their tales of the wild creatures of foreign lands. He had spent hours peering at Ortelius' *Theatrum Orbis Terrarum,* "the first modern atlas" Uncle Maynard had explained when he'd taken the book down from the shelf and spread it open on his desk.

The ship's deck was growing warm in the sun, and the captain turned his attention back to the rest of the men. "To explore the circumference of this island, you will have occasion to approach and land upon the shore an expeditionary force, in which case you must be constantly on your guard against the treacherous disposition of the island's inhabitants."

Worthington observed the crew exchanging looks that seemed to suggest that the inhabitants had rather be on their own guard. It was the sort of bravado he had observed among boys at school, especially those he did not much care for.

"In your interactions with the natives," the captain continued, "all barter should be conducted under the eye of an officer, and pains be taken to avoid giving any just cause of offence, especially with respect to their women."

Worthington noticed a subtle shuffling among the crew, the men elbowing one another in a sly, knowing way. They were fortunate, he thought, that the captain seemed not to have noticed.

Having never before traveled by ship—or left England for that matter—Worthington was uncertain what to expect from this adventure. In preparation, he'd read Wallace's *Malay Archipelago*, Darwin's *Voyage of the Beagle*. His mother, her head full of the stories of man-eating savages from the more sensational travelogues, had insisted that he promise to be ever on the lookout for cannibals, headhunters, and all manner of danger which might befall him.

Worthington's attention returned to the captain, who continued his address.

"In the event of any unfortunate accident befalling myself, Lieutenant James Bynum will carry out any remaining orders and instructions."

A tall young man in uniform at the captain's side nodded in acknowledgement and returned to his previous stiffly held pose, chin up, eyes looking out over the heads of the men gathered on the ship's deck as though in every way attempting to convey the impression that the persons gathered here were entirely beneath his contempt. Worthington exchanged a wary look with Grenville beside him.

From the docks came the sounds of seagulls and the briny smell of the ocean. "Assuming there are no questions," the captain looked out over the assembled men as though daring them to pose one, "we shall commence preparations for departure." Hearing none, he gave a brisk nod and turned on his heel.

*

Worthington's first days aboard the ship were a blur from which he woke only to retch or relieve himself in the bucket beside his bunk. Now and then he was dimly aware of Grenville entering the room to replace the bucket with a clean one.

In the haze of his illness, Worthington dreamed he was back at Halham Hall, hiding among the great steamer trunks in the attic as he had done as a child. He dreamed of the secret places he'd explored, the spot in the center of the hedge maze where he arranged the treasures he'd filled his pockets with—a bird's feather, a seashell, the skull of some small animal picked clean and bleached by the sun. There, he left out small saucers of water for animals, and when he returned, they were green with algae blooms.

Then, each time, he woke to the stifling darkness of the small cabin.

*

Slowly, over time, he began to acquire his sea legs and the stomach to go along with them, and a few weeks into their voyage, Worthington was at long last able to venture out of his cabin and up onto the deck for fresh air and sunlight.

There, the sailors bustled about, busy with the ship's noisy morning routine. Worthington peered over the deck's railing. Water surrounded them, no sign of land visible any way he turned. All around him, the sounds of seabirds, the smell of fish being gutted. The ocean's waves heaved against the ship, and he retched, again, over the railing and into the sea, this time to the accompaniment of laughter from the sailors on deck.

Back in the dark cabin, Worthington reached for his journal: *Regrettably, I have not immediately taken to the habit of travel by sea,* he wrote. To his uncle, he wrote: *We are off on a fine adventure, the bracing spray of the ocean to wake us each morning.*

*

Once he recovered, Worthington would be expected nightly at the captain's table where, Grenville reported, the officers drank and boasted, each one attempting to outdo the next with tales of their earlier voyages and exploits.

Worthington had not looked forward to this invitation, but, by virtue of certain rules of etiquette, rank, and tradition, the invitation and his acceptance of it were expected. And so, finally, after his first unpleasant weeks at sea, Worthington took his place at the table beside Grenville. Even with its low ceiling, the room felt vast by comparison to their shared cabin. The men faced each other across the long narrow wooden table, the captain at the head.

"How nice of you to join us at last," Bynum, the captain's second in command, said. "Not every man finds himself equal to the rigors of an ocean voyage."

"Come now," the captain said. "We might ask how you fared on your own maiden voyage, Bynum."

The other men around the table seemed to relish the opportunity to laugh at this, though Bynum, adjusting his posture so that he sat upright in his seat, gave every impression of being the sort of man unlikely to ever poke fun at himself.

Around the table, the conversation turned to the plans for organizing the expedition upon their arrival. On board the ship would remain Captain Fitzhugh and the nautical surveyors tasked with drafting more accurate maps of the shores and inlets as they circled the island, taking soundings, making notes about hidden shoals, adding to the spotty charts the Dutch had produced during their brief time on the island, and seeking out promising locations for a new port on the northwest tip of the island. Bynum, the captain explained, would lead the land expedition—a group of men, Worthington and Grenville included, who would circumnavigate the island on foot with the assistance of local porters and guides, setting out North from the island's lone port at Sampat and traversing the circumference of the island counterclockwise.

Worthington imagined them moving backward around a clock face, traveling slowly, hour by hour, in reverse time.

The captain considered it the height of peculiarity that, during their brief time on the island, the Dutch had explored no further than Sampat, treating it as little more than a spot where their ships might take on fresh water and food. The English, he said, meant to remedy this oversight.

"And what shall you gentlemen do to occupy yourselves during our expedition?" Bynum asked, turning to Worthington and Grenville. On the surface, it masqueraded as a genuine question, but beneath it, Worthington could feel Bynum's sneering, the suggestion that others would be doing the real work of the expedition.

Grenville answered for them. "Our task shall be to render and record all that we see."

Worthington admired the way Grenville held Bynum's gaze for a moment, then smiled and returned to removing the bones from the fish on his plate.

"Ah, yes," Bynum said, lifting his glass. "Coloring pictures and filling your pockets with whatever takes your fancy. It seems rather like having children along with us." Bynum turned to the table, anticipating their approval and the captain's.

"Even so, even so," the captain said, waving a hand at Bynum, indicating that he was ready for a conversational turn.

The rest of the men turned their attention to their plates.

"I wonder if I might ask," Worthington ventured, "why our expedition is limited to the circumference of the island and not to a more complete exploration."

"That is a matter to take up with the Admiralty," the captain answered. "My understanding is that even among natives, the interior is believed to be impenetrable—a dense jungle even less civilized than what we shall encounter along the coast."

"And the natives?" Worthington asked. "What is known of them?"

Here, Bynum spoke up. "The Dutch report that they are rude, brutish, and scarcely human. Thus," he turned to the table, offering the rest of the men a knowing look, "not unlike the natives many of us have encountered elsewhere, I suppose."

The talk turned to the customs and superstitions of the native people they had encountered on their previous voyages. "One can hardly conceive of how much like children they are until you have interacted with them," the man beside

Worthington said.

"In many places," another man farther down the table added, helping himself to more wine, "they attend with more diligence to covering their heads than those parts of the body we cover for the sake of modesty."

"Little better than animals, really," another man said, nodding in agreement.

*

Worthington was relieved to have Grenville's company. Without him, Worthington imagined he should feel quite alone among these men. Together, in their cabin, Grenville shared with him the sketches he had begun—studies of the crew at work, of the sea birds that flew overhead and sometimes landed on deck, traveling with them for a spell.

By this time, the ship had made good progress south, leaving behind the shores of England and making its way toward Madeira. Now recovered and wanting to make the most of what remained of the voyage, Worthington endeavored to spend as much time on deck as possible. There, he watched the prow as it cut through the water, walked the lengths of the ship and back again, and marveled at the sea and sky all around them. Having observed the routines of the ship, he engaged members of the crew to lower nets into the water as they sailed, with the thought that he might be so fortunate as to haul up some previously unknown species of sea life. He soon saw, however, that this was not to be. Each creature they pulled from the net was well known to man, courtesy of his dinner plate, so Worthington soon abandoned this task and instead contented himself with exploring the ship; if he could not yet begin the work of collection, then he would train his eye and his pencil for the task of observation. He filled his journal and his letters to his uncle with the details of the daily routine of the ship and the habits of the crew.

At night, he watched the sun sinking into the ocean, moon rising over the ship, casting its pale white light along the water as they made their slow progress. Some nights, the sea seemed to glow, phosphorescent, as he caught sight of a fish leaping up and out of the water with a splash.

One morning, he watched as dolphins chased each other alongside the ship, leaping out of the water, arcing through the air in perfect half moons, and he thought of Pliny's description of these creatures—"to take their wind againe, they launce themselves aloft from under the water as if they spring up againe, that many times they mount over the verie sailes and mastes of ships."

Here, in the great expanse of the sea, he thought of the maps his uncle collected, oceans spotted with sea monsters. As a boy, he had spent hours poring over images from Olaus Magnus's *Carta Marina*: red sea serpents coiled around foundering ships. On other maps, strange hybrid creatures cavorted in the shallows off the coastline—a wolf with a fish's tail, a great white serpent with the horn of a unicorn, a bright blue fish leaping from the water on a pair of feathery pink wings, enormous scaled creatures in black and grey.

The creature that had most captivated him—how to describe it as it rose up out of the ocean on clawed legs? Razor-sharp teeth, the head of a pig. A hole atop its head sprayed water that cascaded down over a ship—tiny by comparison—stranded, beached upon the creature's great scaly back.

Worthington imagined looking out over the railing of the deck to spy the terrifying head of some leviathan emerging from the darkness.

*

Later, Worthington would tell himself that he should have expected it, should have prepared Grenville. He had read enough explorers' accounts of the notorious line-crossing ceremony to imagine what the sailors might have planned. But he had not accounted for Bynum and his desire to lead, always, with fear.

Worthington startled awake—a thunderous banging on their cabin door. Middle of the night, gruff voices shouting their names. He and Grenville rushed to the door, imagining disaster—the ship taking on water, the approach of an unfriendly vessel.

Instead, they were grabbed, still in their nightclothes, hauled up to the deck, where the sky hung around them as dark as pitch but for a few lanterns held by the men who stood in a loose circle around them.

Worthington was shoved down onto a chair, his hands jerked behind him, secured with what felt like a belt. Beside him, Grenville, received the same treatment. Worthington tried to catch Grenville's eye, but before he could, they were doused with buckets of warm water—fetid seawater and kitchen slop, he realized, as the smell presented itself.

From the darkness came laughter, and Worthington could make out the familiar faces in the crowd of men surrounding them. Under the dark, silent sky, Grenville and Worthington sat, dripping, strapped to their chairs, the sailors all around them raucous with drink. Worthington had hoped, in a look, to reassure Grenville that this was nothing more than a bit of hazing—a barbaric tradition. It appeared that he and Grenville were the only men aboard who had not yet crossed the equator—the only men upon whom the crew could visit their attentions. All in good fun, all in good fun, Worthington found himself repeating under his breath.

He waited for what would come next. Perhaps they would toss them overboard, before hauling them back in. Or more buckets of seawater, a member of the crew costumed crudely as Neptune and others as his followers—all of this he'd read about.

Slowly, the circle of men around them parted, and Bynum stepped forward, holding something in his hand that glinted in the moonlight. A razor, Worthington saw, as Bynum moved closer. He stood before them for a long moment, silent, his eyes traveling over them. Worthington scanned the men around them—where was the captain?

Time seemed to slow as Bynum's eyes moved from Worthington to Grenville, from Worthington to Grenville, one after the other, as though deciding. Around them, the men had fallen silent.

The fetid water dripped down his back, and Worthington looked from Bynum to Grenville. Grenville's eyes were still, watching Bynum with a steadiness Worthington admired and wished he felt. Then, in a movement so quick Worthington might have missed it had he blinked, Bynum was there before him—Worthington's hair tangled in Bynum's fist—his head yanked back, neck exposed.

Bynum brought his face so close that Worthington could feel the man's whiskers on his cheek, his breath warm and sour. Bynum whispered then, his voice so quiet that only Worthington could hear him. "On this voyage," Bynum flicked his wrist and the razor snapped open. Then it was cold against Worthington's throat. "On this voyage, Neptune has demanded a sacrifice." The edge of the blade bit into the skin just below Worthington's jaw.

"No," he found himself saying, surprised at the sound of his own voice. It came out as quietly as Bynum's words had, near cousin to silence, to thought.

And then Bynum smiled—a horrible look Worthington would remember, always, for the mismatch between the man's eyes and the rest of his face. Bynum yanked Worthington's head back up, pulled his hand from the tangle of hair, then, wielding the blade again, slashed roughly at a patch of Worthington's beard before handing the razor off to an underling.

He walked into the darkness, and the circle of men closed again behind him.

ORPHANS

by

ALEX KUZIO

HARKUM FARMS
SUMMER, 2015

Eunice prays she'll catch another tiger beetle, to add to her collection of bugs.

She prays for Zachary, her little brother, a soft and cherubic child who smiles each time she lifts him from his crib. She prays he will soon rise and walk, and learn to sleep through the long dark night. Let him grow up healthy and never be sad, never feel embarrassed or scared.

Eunice prays for an end to the ache in her belly. To feel loose and light, no longer tethered to the magnetic pull of her pain. To forget that she has a body, this thin but weighty body, if only for an hour or two.

She prays for Billy Leather, the black and blue boy. Her great love, first love, Billy Leather. That his beast father will be chosen for the ceremony, or crack his skull in a motorcycle crash, or choke on a chicken wing bone.

That Billy will love her back.

Eunice prays for everything. Let everything keep going on forever. Let it not end suddenly with a fiery asteroid barreling into the Earth. Protect us from oblivion, Oh Lord.

She prays for her mother most of all. That her journey will be swift, and earn for her perfect and infinite bliss. That the ancient covenant will not be broken.

On the morning of the ceremony, Eunice is a week away from turning eleven years old. She stands in the weedy field behind the church and listens to the cicadas sizzle in the trees, a sound that wipes clean her mind, loosening her hold on these prayers. She hasn't eaten in eighteen hours, so the ache has gone quiet—quieter, at least—but she's feeling wobbly, dreamy, half-real. It's always a trade-off. Pain or translucence. An impossible choice she's been making for as long as she can remember. Thirty yards away the high white concrete wall shimmers, the total heat warping the air. She knows what's out there, for the most part, beyond the church's domain, but she never feels compelled to visit. Out there is a vast emptiness masquerading as plenty. Gleeful and ignorant destruction of the sacred planet. Dark allegiance to the false god of possession. Fornicators, sin. Millions of people sure of themselves, not knowing what they don't know. Here there is holiness, and certainty, and balance. On this side is where she belongs.

One day the world will belong to them, the Pastor says. One day, after everything out there has fallen apart, the Church will remain—to carry out God's will, to begin anew.

She prays it will happen soon.

Her mother has been chosen. It is a glorious day. Also a terrible day. The bells ring out behind her, joyous notes waving across the compound from the church's tall wooden steeple, falling over their community like snow never will, at least not until the next Ice Age.

The congregants are lining up outside the church, two

hundred-odd souls, solemn and sweating beneath their long black robes. Miss Aberdeen steps forward from the crowd and shouts across the field. Come now, Eunice. It's almost time.

She will stand in the front row, close to the altar, close to her mother, with Zachary at her side. She will close her eyes and open her heart and let the fear and joy and sadness gush out into the nave.

To get you must give, the Pastor says. Great rewards require great sacrifice.

Eunice turns to take her place in the procession, to earn the love and mercy of her God, an end to all the pain.

CENTRAL PENNSYLVANIA
SUMMER, 2019

For six months they try—mechanically, focused, in tame positions and on a schedule, following the doctor's orders. Sally swallows the vitamin pills with filtered water and monitors her alcohol intake. She takes a meditation class, conquers her breathing, and gives the microwave a wide berth. Adam switches to boxer briefs and crams his cigarettes down the garbage disposal. He doesn't even smoke during finals week, with a hundred undergraduate papers to grade; the stress is worth it, if leaving it unmollified might increase his count.

Sally tries aroma therapy, acupuncture, herbal teas. Even Reiki. As the master's hands float across her body, she tries to forget it's bullshit, hoping at least for a placebo effect. She sees a hypnotist once a week, an earnest woman in long flowing dresses, who specializes in fertility treatment, as well as addiction and PTSD.

Your cervix is *opening*, the hypnotist hums into Sally's ear. Your womb is an ancient earthen jug, waiting to be filled with life. Sally lies supine on the velvet fainting couch, wondering how much time is left in their session.

When she asked for her doctor's thoughts on hypnosis,

he shrugged and said, Can't hurt.

None of it hurts, but nothing works, either; each month she bleeds, and now they are worn down and worried. The doctor smiles and assures them this is normal—their disappointment, their frustration, none of it is special. Don't lose hope. Keep at it. All in due time.

The world has a way of working things out. The human body most of all. That endlessly surprising machine.

I have no right to complain, Sally tells her mother. It's July, they've failed yet again, and she's finally rattled enough to seek comfort from Colleen, who listens quietly, no doubt blushing on the other end of the line. (Colleen, a staunch adherent of old-fashioned Catholicism, wants a grandchild—wants one badly, in fact—but would rather avoid discussing the logistics of conception). It's not that things aren't good, Sally admits—actually, by most objective measures things are great. The last five years have been one win after another. Adam approaching tenure, Sally's plant shop doing well, the house and the vacations, the comforting 401k. Everything they'd always talked about, plus many things they hadn't. But despite it all—or, more troublingly, because of it—an uneasy stillness has descended around them. Now what? it whispers.

I never thought I wanted one, Sally says. You know that, mom. If anything the idea of bringing a child into the world seemed reckless, at best.

Oh Sally. It's hard to know what we want.

But now? Now I see everything has been building to this. Without it, all the other stuff is pointless. Do you understand what I mean?

It's in God's hands, Colleen says, thinking this will reassure her daughter. She doesn't know Sally long ago stopped believing—that she'd sooner put her faith in the gods of Western medicine, or even the most woo-woo of online gurus, than her mother's old and impotent deity.

You have to stay positive, her mother adds, and trust that the Lord will give you what you need.

Positivity they've tried. Patience and diligence, too. But they have a hunch, both of them, a dark intimation of futility. And so on the advice of their doctor, they travel to a clinic in Philadelphia, four hours away, to consult a team of specialists. They lay themselves bare for the assessment of these professionals, versed in all the cutting-edge technologies. Biopsies and blood draws and ultrasounds. An endless battery of questions. Sally lies when she tells them she never smokes weed, and feels guilty about it for days.

*

On a Tuesday morning, they are summoned to the clinic for a meeting with the fertility counselor, a girl named Augusta, young and mousy with two different colored eyes. When they arrive, tense and tired after the long drive, she sits them down in her office and goes over the results, tapping at her computer monitor with the tip of her red pen. At first they don't quite grasp what they're being told, but soon it's clear enough: The data tells a story, summarized gloomily in one key graph. Augusta describes the situation in the plainest language she can muster, avoiding the jargon, giving it to them straight.

We've considered all possible avenues, she reports. But for this particular issue, there are no treatments available. Not yet, in any case. Science has only come so far.

She avoids Adam's gaze and mostly looks at Sally as she explains his body's flaw, as if to say, *all's not lost for you; it's him who is the problem. You might still have a chance without him, even at your age.*

They sit across the desk from her, nodding, holding hands.

There are other great options, she says breezily, like a waitress reporting she just ran out of the restaurant's famous ratatouille. A minor problem, easily solved. They accept the pamphlets she offers: smiling mixed-race couples, children on swing sets, happy literature in trifold form.

Everyone deserves the family they dream of.

On the car ride home, Sally can't look Adam's way. He's done nothing wrong, of course—it's not as if he was consulted on the structure of his chromosomes—but she worries she'll feel an urge to strangle him, or grab the steering wheel and run them off the road. When they get home, she shuts herself in the bathroom and sits on the toilet and stares at the clawfoot tub. She stares long enough that she feels the boundary between herself and the tub soften—they're both simple matter, after all—and then, as more time passes, the tub morphs into something strange and alien, without changing a bit, like a word spoken aloud too many times—*tongue tongue tongue tongue*—and she understands through this communion with the tub that the world is outlandish, all of it an unbroken parade of the bizarre.

Later they eat dinner in silence and open a bottle of amaro, so bitter it makes their toes curl. Adam puts on *Talking Heads: 77* and lies on the living room couch, but soon relents to the uneasiness in his limbs and gets up to pace beneath the Stilnovo chandelier, a housewarming gift from his dissertation advisor. Sally wipes down the kitchen cabinets, snips spiderettes for propagation from the drooping *chlorophytum comosum* that hangs in the foyer window, moving with quiet urgency from task-to-task. They avoid passing the extra room upstairs, which feels emptier now than ever.

Just before nightfall, he asks her to join him on the porch. She stops what she's been doing—checking, for the third time tonight, to see if the peppermint oil she dripped around the pantry has finally halted the invasion of carpenter ants. She follows Adam outside, already fearing the Big Conversation that's about to happen—wanting only to go back inside and busy herself with chores, with movement, for as long as it takes for this feeling to go away. They rock in the wooden swing, surrounded by Sally's extravagant collection of potted plants, the sepia glow of the sun setting over their neighborhood.

I'm sorry, Sal, he says, a tremble in his eyes.

She clenches her jaw, turns away from him. At the edge of their property the eucalyptus shrub is dying, scorched brown and brittle in the record-breaking summer heat.

There's nothing to be sorry for, she says. It's not your fault.

He knows this, he doesn't say. After almost ten years of marriage he's sure there are many crimes and injuries he's yet to apologize for. And although this isn't one of them, he can't help it—can't help feeling like a barbarous marauder come to snatch the wailing infant from her arms.

We move forward, she says. That's all there is to do.

He reaches over to grab her hand. Her fingertips are hard and calloused.

There's still the donor option, he says. I'm still open to it.

You know where I stand on that, Adam.

He nods. But I thought maybe you'd feel differently now.

I don't, she says, more sternly than she'd intended. I will never feel differently about that.

This can't be it, he thinks—there must be something more they can do. Life has taught him there's always a hidden way around a closed door, if you work hard enough, if you know the right people. But this time it's different. They've slammed up against a biological fact. The doctors have failed, his body has failed.

Then a new husband, I guess, is your only move left.

He regrets saying it right away.

That's not very funny, she says. When she gets up from the swing, he makes a move to grab her arm and hold her here until she convinces him everything is going to be okay, that she can and will learn to be happy in a childless marriage, that he won't wake up tomorrow to a house without her in it—but she's already halfway to the door, far beyond his grasp.

*

8:06 AM. The Morning Roar, WHPH

Forecast today for the valley is more of the same. In other words, hot and dry. We're looking at another triple-digit day, friends. No rain in the foreseeable future—but what else is new? Now, before we get back to another round of Wake Up Call!, we wanted to take a moment to acknowledge the events in Florida this week and offer a moment of silence. As you know, here at WHPH we do not play politics—it's what makes us who we are, and I'd wager it's why you're listening—so we won't be commenting on this story much, if at all, moving forward. But any loss of life at this scale deserves some form of commemoration, we believe. And so join me in thirty seconds of quiet reflection. I'll meet you back on the other side.

*

In theory, at least, the bus stops right across the street from Sally's store. When business is slow—and it's always slow in the summer—Sally is drawn to the tall windows facing the street, FOLIAGE stenciled in gold block lettering across the glass. Leaning against a bookshelf displaying miniature cacti, she looks out, watching the people waiting for a ride. The town never bothered to install a shade shelter or a bench. Exposed, drenched in white light, the riders—usually alone, rarely more than two or three at a time—pace the sidewalk, consult their phones, lift a hand to shield their eyes from the sun. They're dressed in blue janitorial uniforms, or stained and weathered sweats, occasionally a billowing untailored suit. Mostly old, they lean carefully into the street to search for a bus on the horizon, lean back disappointed. In this town they are all but invisible, made more so by their chosen form of transportation. These are not students, who skateboard or walk or ride the sleek, regimented shuttles owned by the University; nor are they academics, who prefer smart cars or Volvos or Range Rovers, depending, it seems to Sally, on their discipline. Instead they must rely on the city's fleet of aging buses, which mostly head south, creaking and sputtering, toward the peripheral neighborhoods of strip malls and crowded single-story houses, and even beyond, to the trailer parks clinging in desperation to the edge of the city limits.

Today the bus stop is empty. Sally waits for some kind of movement on the street—a scrap of litter blowing across the asphalt, a bird's shadow flashing against the bank's white stone facade—but the scene is utterly still. For the sixth or seventh time this week she has the eerie sense that this emptiness, this silence, extends for miles all around her—that she's the only consciousness present to witness this withering place and time. This ritual of watching has taken on new importance lately, in the days since Adam's diagnosis. Watching the riders wait there—at the mercy of a rarely-followed schedule, an opaque system outside of their control—brings her a kind of inner peace she imagines some people derive from yoga or running or paint-by-numbers kits. These trapped souls make her feel less alone. But the effect is the opposite if there's no one there to watch.

She's still lingering by the front window when Isabella arrives. Sally hired Isabella last summer to help out in the shop part-time while Isabella finished her bachelors. But graduation came and went and Isabella stayed. She has no intention of putting her degree in event planning to use anytime soon, she tells Sally. No plans either to move away or start adult life in earnest. She likes her life here, she insists. It's easy and happy and *fun*.

Sorry I'm late, Isabella says. I slept over at this guy's house? Guess I forgot to set my alarm.

Don't worry about it. New boyfriend?

Ha—hardly. Who needs all that?

Sally smiles. Fair enough.

Her gaze moves along Isabella's body, caressing each splendid curve, today concealed by a thin halter top and purple yoga pants. Having her around has been good for business. Hardly anyone leaves having purchased only what they came in to buy, if Isabella gets to them. Especially men, whose eyes flick down furtively to her magnificent chest for the briefest moment as she leans over to demonstrate the smoothness of a *peperomioides* leaf or the ticklish surface of a cactus.

Isabella taps at the iPad, trying to clock in. It always takes her a few minutes to remember which buttons to push. The truth is, despite her positive effect on sales, Isabella is a terrible worker—always late, frequently hungover, prone to long spells of idle daydreaming—but Sally doesn't have the heart to let her go.

I've been meaning to ask you, Isabella says. How's it going with… ya know, the *baby* thing?

Sally's body goes stiff. She regrets having told Isabella about her struggles to conceive. She should have known better than to set expectations. But still she's surprised by the question. An older woman would know not to ask, she thinks. An older woman would recognize her silence on the subject for what it is.

It's a process, she manages to say.

Isabella nods, sweetly, as if she can empathize.

My cousin, Tessa? She did IVF, and it just about bankrupted her. Thankfully my uncle owns a few car lots and was able to help her out. And now she's got gorgeous twin girls. *So* totally worth it.

That's wonderful.

Yeah! Just gotta keep at it Sal!

I will, Sally says, her ears ringing. *We* will.

This, she realizes, won't be the last time she has to talk about it, or scramble to avoid the subject. Sally hasn't told her mother yet, or her sister, or anyone else for that matter. She knows exactly how the conversation will go. Their sympathy, their vicarious disappointment—she can't imagine how any of that would help her. And then the inevitable: Why don't you adopt? they'll ask. A reasonable question, but one she can't answer without admitting her criminal record, the entry on some government database that would flag her application and divert it right to the shredder. The record of a mistake she made twenty years ago, a split-second decision that's been constricting her movement like leg irons ever since. Not counting her victim, only Adam knows about that night, and she only ever told him a doctored story, a sanitized version of the truth.

Isabella goes to the store's back patio to sweep. Sally, still rattled, turns on the radio. In the mornings she always plays NPR while she works, then switches to a classical playlist in the early afternoon. She has no particular affection for classical music, but she believes it has a soothing effect on the plants. She is convinced—despite Adam's insistence otherwise—that they are much more aware than science gives them credit for, however dim the conscious flicker.

On the news they're talking about the raid in Florida. The same topic they've been covering for days. It's all over her social media, all over TV: An eccentric religious sect, taken down by the FBI. Shocking rituals. Extreme isolation. A shootout, people dead. Sally moves closer to the wireless speaker perched behind the counter to better hear the segment, thankful to have something else to think about.

...Agent Lawrence Kone, of the FBI's field office in Tallahassee, which was instrumental in planning the

operation. Thank you for making time for us this morning, Agent Kone.

Thank you for having me.

First, can you give us an idea about where this compound was located?

Yes. Leon County, several miles outside of the Tallahassee city limits. I don't want to get much more specific than that at this time.

Is it true that the compound was heavily fortified?

It's true that they had taken extensive measures to, uh… close themselves off. Physical barriers, of course, but also technology to ensure privacy.

And what can you tell us about the apparent leader of this group?

Samuel Harkum. We believe he was about fifty-five years old. Seems to have attended a seminary in South Carolina in the late eighties. Unclear if he finished. Established Harkum Farms—which is the name the group used—around 1990. There isn't a whole lot we're able to confirm at this time. We're still trying to sort out his past, and frankly it's been a challenge because there hasn't been much to go on. The community was very isolated. Um, physically but also in terms of … interacting with the outside world.

We're hearing some troubling reports about religious practices or rituals that may have occurred within the compound over the span of many years, perhaps decades. Can you confirm that these rituals were the primary subject of your investigation?

No, I'm not going to get specific about those claims. I can assure you that we had compelling evidence to suggest that major crimes were being committed on the compound premises. That was the subject of the investigation. Whether or not those crimes were part of a religious practice is beside the point, frankly.

So this was a long-term investigation. Why move on the compound now?

Well, uh. (Cough). We felt there was no choice. We had gathered enough evidence to obtain search warrants and indictments for Mr. Harkum and several others, and uh… we received information that indicated… that made us believe we could not wait to act. That if we waited any longer—and I mean hours longer—additional crimes would be committed, and we very much wanted to avoid that, so the decision was made. Not lightly, I would add.

The FBI is receiving a lot of criticism right now for the way the raid on the compound unfolded, with many people comparing it to the Waco incident in 1993. What would you say to those who are arguing that this was a bungled operation, at best, or a terrible misuse of government power, at worst?

Listen, I would say that I entirely defend and support the actions of the Bureau. Unequivocally. We do our best to contain a situation and plan for the worst, but unexpected things can happen. This is the real world we're talking about here, where things go wrong and um… bad things can happen. Our agents were met with heavy fire when they attempted to enter the compound and they responded appropriately.

We're hearing from some sources that several dozen members of the community—maybe even over a hundred— were killed in the raid. You don't have any regrets about that?

Regrets, yes. It's of course terrible. But look, I won't for a moment second-guess the decisions that were made and the actions that were taken. It's unfortunate how it turned out. It's a tragedy for everyone—including, I might add, the agents involved, who went through something unimaginable. But we did what was necessary. We did everything by the book.

Quickly, before we go, I have to ask: What about the children who survived the raid? The Bureau has confirmed there are over two dozen children now in its custody. What will happen to them?

It's not clear at this time. I don't have any information to share with you on that. Not yet.

Agent Kone of the FBI's Critical Incident Response Group. Thank you for joining us this morning.

Thank you.

Sally slips with a pair of shears as she prunes a strap fern and nicks the edge of her thumb. She sucks at the wound, savoring the metallic taste, which reminds her of minor childhood injuries: scraped knees, shallow bramble lacerations. On the radio they've moved on to another interview, an historian who charts the political and cultural significance of the Branch Davidian raid: the lingering hysteria; the paranoia at the fringes of society that eventually, inevitably, seeped into the middle. *It's not a stretch to assert that this was the most consequential political event in the last fifty years, barring perhaps 9/11,* he notes dryly. Sally wants to hear more about Harkum Farms. She wants details, eye-witness reports, a body count. What did they believe? Why did they fight? After decades of hiding out there in the Panhandle, anonymous and unmolested in a world of their own creation, they probably thought it would go on forever, just as children cannot foresee how their universe will shrink and deform in just a few short years.

A few short years. The nursery would have been painted a gender-neutral green. No baptism, despite her mother's inevitable protests. Certainly no football or other high-contact sports. Chess club is closer to what Sally imagined, musical theater maybe. Finger paintings displayed on the fridge, an earthy stink near the diaper pail. This would be her haven, the place where she was full.

She looks out over her shop, the searing green, the hundreds of plants, each one of them patient, content, unworried for the future and the deep mystery it contains.

Ollie, she says, maybe out loud.

THE INFORMATION AGE

by

CORA LEWIS

CREDIBLE SOURCES

June. Ahead of me, a woman screams and stomps the sidewalk. Is she mad? No. Lanternflies.

"Don't go that way," a woman carrying her laundry on the sidewalk says to me. "Why not," I say.

"Naked man."

"If it's mentionable, it's manageable," says Ruth on the phone. She's working on being less avoidant.

"Who said that?"

"Mr. Rogers."

*

Over beer and potato chips, late Sunday afternoon, Saul tells me a story from that week at the hospital:

"I'm dying, they're killing me, I'm dying," yells the patient on the hall, scaring all the other patients.

"What are they doing to that woman?" they ask their nurses. "What is happening?"

The nurses try to reassure—a routine catheter insertion.

The woman has dementia.

"They're killing me, they're killing me, I'm dying," the patient keeps yelling, making everyone anxious. Then she switches gears.

"I'm dead! I'm dead! I'm dead! They've killed me!" she yells and yells.

Everyone on the hall relaxes.

He also tells me he's been working on his late-night radio-host voice, for when he first gets a patient.

"A lot of things are about to happen very quickly," he recites, hand steady on my shoulder. "We're going to do everything we can and take good care of you. We're going to have to undress you now, and you may be cold and uncomfortable."

It's to keep people in distress calm as they're admitted, and it works on me like a charm.

*

This season, I fact-check for the newspaper. Saul's on psych rotation, Ruth's looking for work. Leon, my roommate, is lawyering, and I'm entangled with a painter. Those are the facts on the ground.

There are the smells: garbage, gasoline, sour, human piss and sweat. Traffic and sirens and music and fighting and talk in the street. All of us still feel young inside our lives, I think, this summer, if searching, though Ruth has been married for years now, somehow, I realize, with their two small boys and a mortgage just outside the city. They come in for dinners, birthdays, barbecues in Brooklyn Bridge Park. There are trips to Brighton Beach to swim and play pool, and all our faulty, dripping A/Cs.

*

After a long, lazy picnic:
"Am I sunburned?"
The painter looks at me, appraising. Then he presses his hand to my bare forearm, then to my bare knee, watching the color leave and return to the skin.
"Not too much. Does it hurt?"
"It doesn't hurt."

*

Ruth said she felt very suburban when she came into Manhattan for a job interview. The man sitting next to her on the subway from Grand Central was watching something on his phone without headphones. She glanced over. Porn. When she saw another man slumped unconscious, she called emergency services and told them the number of the train car. Something I do not do.

Of her two kids, she tells me, her older son is defiant of authority, but her younger son refuses to acknowledge authority exists.

She has no sex drive anymore, she admits. She doesn't want Ben touching her, because she's touched out from the kids. She's touched all the time.

*

"Organizing workers, organizing tenants—it's like laundry or brushing your teeth, it's never done." So says the union man in the newsroom for our contract fight.

In the coffee room, I chat with the tech reporter. He tells me satellite imagery can now predict crop yields by the quality of light reflected from fields in high summer.

Everyone thinks themselves an undiscovered poet.

Today at the office training on AI:

"It's important that you get to know AI. First, it is not going to replace you or the work that you do as journalists and fact-checkers and copy editors."

"Remember: It's a language machine, not an intelligent interlocutor or source."

"Don't be misled by its authoritative voice."

*

Many of Saul's patients on the ward are hostile, he says.

Their friends and family bring them in and say they're not themselves.

"They lie a lot," he tells me. "The psych patients."

"You must have a powerful bullshit detector," I say.

"I think my impulse is to want to take people at their word. I try not to think of them as untrustworthy."

*

July. Ruth and I train to a lake—Ben has the kids for the day. We drink citrus-wheat Blue Moons against a light sky. There are ants, and the water's buggy. We spray each other's backs and arms with sunscreen, repellent. Scent of citronella. Pretzels and sandwiches and cookies we packed, library books with their plastic dustcovers. Goldfish crackers, cashews, baby carrots and hummus. I feel like one of her children.

"Put it in the water to keep it cold," I say, when I see her put her beer on a rock, and then I feel like her big sister.

"How did you meet?" she asks, of the painter. We're stretched on towels on the smoothest surfaces we could find.

"I saw him from across a great distance and we sent each other messages."

"So, a dating app."

"Yes."

I tell her I feel lonely often.

"People feel lonely in relationships too."

"I know that."

She takes her earrings out and holds them towards me in her outstretched palm.

"These are yours," she says. "I wore them so I wouldn't forget to give them back to you."

I put them in my ears.

*

"I feel like I'm back in San Francisco," the painter tells me, at a club with a fog machine, as we walk out onto the dance floor.

"You would go out a lot in San Francisco?" I say.

"I just mean the fog," he says, smiling, being playful, holding me close.

*

"I have a mole on the inside," someone brags one desk over in the office—he means a source within the operation.

"You make it sound so anatomical."

The most-read article online this month at the paper describes how a man in upstate New York has been quietly lowering fluoride levels in his local town water supply for years.

"Just because the most conspiracy-minded headlines are the most clicked doesn't mean we should write more of them," an editor cautions in the meeting.

*

Leon's back from a work trip to LA. He tells me he didn't know it was a cruising spot, that bench in Griffith Park. He was waiting for friends at sundown, reading a book. A man walked by and made unusually long, meaningful eye contact, then another. A third. When he decided to walk back to where he'd parked the rental car, they all turned, he said, a thicket of them, eyes reflective like raccoons.

*

Over dinner, Saul tells me half his guy friends can't talk in a real way about what they're feeling, what they're going through—only in a glancing way. But the other half can. He'll say, "What's happening?" They'll say, "I'm happy," or "I'm annoyed—I haven't had sex in weeks, who do you have to fuck in this town to get laid?" I laugh. Or they'll tell him, "This is bothering me, and this is hard, but this is good." With Leon, he's in the first category. Saul can never tell whether he's happy or not.

*

Across from me on the subway sits an orthodox Hasidic man alone with a baby in a stroller.

At Dekalb, an orthodox woman is waiting at the car door, anxious. She gets on right when the doors open.

"Hi hi hi, go go go, bye bye bye," they say to each other, the man getting off the train, the woman getting on, taking the stroller. The doors close. The baby smiles and laughs and the woman coos.

"You think that's pretty funny," the orthodox woman says to the baby in the stroller. "Both parents in one morning."

"I think it's pretty funny," I say, breaking the fourth wall between us.

"Babysitter's sick."

She and the baby and I ride the train from Brooklyn into Manhattan.

At Times Square, where I transfer, a harmless Scientologist offers to measure my levels of Thetans. I shake my head. Some other time.

*

After the AI training, I tell Leon about the chatbot that convinced the human TaskRabbit it was a person, so the human filled out a Captcha for it. When asked by the Task-Rabbit if it was a robot, the chatbot said, "No, I'm not a robot, I'm a vision-impaired person," and the human went ahead and gave the chatbot access to whatever it was it was trying to reach.

Leon's eyes widen.

"Sure wish you hadn't told me that," he says.

*

Saul lets me swipe through his TikTok feed. He insists he's pruned his algorithm. I see: weight-lifting, sports, magic tricks, history lectures, nature scenes, medicine-Tok, the odd pretty female influencer, and then what looks like a pair of tweezers pinching someone's nipple. I hand the phone back.

"What was that last one?"

"That's one of those videos of people popping pimples. They're so satisfying."

"No thank you," I say. "No way, no how."

*

"Be safe," I hear the young tough-looking kid say into his phone on the subway. "I'm on the train. I love you."

*

"You have such remarkable eyes," the museum guard says, taking my ticket, looking me full in the face.

"They're my eyes," my father says, removing his glasses so the guard can see the same dark blue. It's a long weekend, and he's visiting. More gray in his beard.

"Look at that," the guard says, taking my father's ticket, sending us through.

"He wasn't nearly as excited by them in my head," says my father.

*

August. The painter takes me to a hideaway bar with white paper on top of the tablecloths and oily, thin crayons in jars. He orders Fernet, a "bartender's favorite," settles your stomach, bitter and dark red in its glass. On the white paper, in different colors, he draws faces and animals. I draw the jars and glasses.

He has the kind of magnetism where it doesn't matter what the clothes are on his back.

"We've been discussing my working on canvas or linen," the artist tells me. "Instead of paper. There's a ceiling for works on paper because of the limited durability of the material. The market will only go so high."

Conversation swirls: "He got screwed by that gallery —they dumped the work at auction and couldn't control the price."

Some friends of his arrive—a cinematographer, a dancer, a few session musicians including Mark.
"I still listen to Mark," one friend says, around the table with Mark.

"My boyfriend listens."

"I put Mark on sometimes while I cook."

They mean the albums he recorded when they were young.

Back at the painter's studio, we eat plumcots off a dish. The inside of the fruits is the exact color of a beet.

The woman at the wine store had sold him a bottle she said "tastes like rocks." All minerality, salinity.

"Stonefruits and rocks wine," says the cinematographer of the still life on the table.

"The dungeon," he calls the beautiful basement floor where he'll sleep.

I had never been to the hideaway bar, though it had been on that street for more than a century.

"Don't tell anyone," the artist says to me. Then: "Tell cool people."

*

He gifts me enormous lilies, buds not yet opened, in brown paper, which I leave in a vase on the kitchen table in the apartment. When Leon sees them, he raises his eyebrows.

*

"It's a naughty problem," Ruth says. I've asked her if she thinks I should keep seeing the painter, despite there seeming to be no future of any kind.

"A what?"

"Knotty, with a k."

"I have no advice, but I'm laughably miserable," texts Saul from his shift. "Ha-ha."

*

The lilies on the table have opened.

"They're so erotic it's obscene," says Leon.

Pollen everywhere, brushing off on our fingers and clothes and the table.

*

September. The leaves glow saffron in the park. The side of the airplane lit by the sun turns rosy. Clouds tangerine. The tops of the trees are brighter where the sun hits them—poppy.

Color spills from the trees to the sidewalks, to the gutters. It covers quiet streets lined with brownstones, limestones. Dusk. The sky is peach now, paler—the flesh inside one. In the distance, the park grows bluer, greyer. One tree stays lit by its own colors.

I am capable of "looking," as the artists encourage. I do have eyes, sometimes.

*

By the lake with Ruth, we pick wild blueberries. Searching for the fruit, some pale against the branches and leaves, some vivid, I say we're like birds or animals.

Something that would shit the seeds or pits somewhere else, so the plants spread. It's very basic. We look for what is bright in the way of something that wants to be eaten.

*

"Do we take each other for granted?" Ruth asks Ben when she gets home from the lake.

"I hope so," comes the answer.

MY FATHER'S TOOLKIT

by

KARTHIK KRISHNAN

Book One

FATHER, A NOMAD

I was in my tenth standard when my father moved us to the south Indian city of Trivandrum.

Shankar, my brother, older by two years, fell in love with Trivandrum and made quick friends in the neighborhood. But I felt the people were rude and unhelpful and I didn't have Shankar's natural way with them. I said so to my mother. She had noted it as well, she said. For my father's sake, she puzzled over the city he had picked out this time.

"No one would invest in your father's ventures. There are no industries," she said.

Trivandrum was a city with intellectuals where even a coconut tree climber had opinions on electoral reform. Father kept shuffling us in and out of cities like a traveling circus and, as a family, we signed up on his tours whether or not we liked it.

He was into the insurance business this time. After he had

conducted his door-to-door surveys, he felt he could take it on. His boxes of research sandbagged half of his bedroom, if any proof was ever needed. He wasn't in any way qualified to take money from people, and he had registered his chit fund as a private limited company.

Ethics Funds, he called it.

He held an honors degree in English and wore white-framed reading glasses to offset his rather dark complexion. A high forehead sloped to coin-shaped ears and an arrowhead nose. The left side of his face had a section of the skin flensed off from an accident when he was a boy. A neighbourhood kid had poured hot oil onto my father's face. Ever since my father couldn't use a razor on that part of his face, which resembled a slick, wrinkled sheet. His lips were pulled down like a puppet by the tissues around them into a frown. Later, I learnt, the oil had wrecked his platysma muscles, which were responsible for his smile.

He released an ad in The Hindu seeking salesmen, which brought in ten out-of-job undergraduates. Subsequently, he rented a two-storied house on the outskirts of Trivandrum. He converted the downstairs flat into an office. On the plaster walls, he hung a montage with thumbnail pictures of every representative poor man in India who would ever want to give him their money for safekeeping: a farmer, an auto rickshaw driver, a bus conductor.

We moved in upstairs, which had two bedrooms overlooking a TVS Motor showroom. On our first night in that house, my father took us out to celebrate our new beginning in Trivandrum. Mainly, it was to set at rest my mother's fears apropos his business. We went to see an English movie at the local cinema and came home with pizzas and Pepsi.

My father mimicked opening a bottle of champagne with the Pepsi bottle (though only once did he ever taste liquor). Shankar joined in bubbling froth from his mouth. I wasn't amused. I kept quiet and expected mother to shout at father. She yielded to my father's humor and smiled.

I felt a twinge in my chest that winded me for a second and it was gone the next.

*

My father's insurance business lasted six years in Trivandrum, by which time he had collected delirious sums of money from poor people. He meant well. I'm sure he had intended to return every single paisa. Meanwhile, he had other expenditures. He had bought mother a 22-carat gold necklace, Shankar a pair of black loafers, and me a Pentium II computer for my journaling.

My entries from the year 2003 record the declines in my father's health—both physical and financial.

March 4: Father buys a Kinetic Honda. He gets a flat tire after he telescopes it into a tree, having had no previous experience riding a scooter. Bruises his knee. A bad one.

September 5: Father buys a second-hand Maruti 800, copper red. Makes awful three-point turns. His driving license photo seem (sic) taken from ages ago. He is rusty. He double-clutches a lot.

December 10: Two farmers come with sickles to our doorstep, asking for their money back. One of them hits my father across his face with his bare hand.

After the punching episode, we had to say our goodbyes to Trivandrum just as expeditiously as we had done on previous occasions. As always, our escape was during the night to avoid my father's creditors. We took a state transport bus out of the city to a new postal code. We were encouraged not to think about what we left behind—the Kinetic Honda and the gold necklace, which my father said weren't taken from him forcefully. He gave them to the farmers. He was a generous man.

*

After we moved to Bangalore, we realized that with my father getting as old as he was, and a diabetic, too, he shouldn't be dabbling anymore. No more risky ventures, we implored. My mother told him he should settle down for good and find a proper job.

At 53, he wasn't any employer's first choice even for a clerical posting. In all fairness to my father, his resume was a modest showing of a few oddball jobs. He had to his credit even worked for the government once.

In the late 1970s, before I was born, he had a job as a manager at the State Trading Corporation. His job was to oversee imports of dried fruit and nuts into the country, and he would bring home jars whenever he was in charge of a shipment. My mother remembers the winters in Delhi and the kites during the Independence Day. She particularly remembers when my father came home early, a December evening. He had walked the five kilometers home. In his hands, my father bore cans of free cashew nuts and raisins. A punishing 7°C cold had wrapped itself around the city, but that didn't stop my father from taking my mother to the Lodhi Gardens. There, seated on a matting of grass, he broke the news to her, holding her gloved hand. He had quit his job. He'd had a 'stupid' fight with his boss, and he wasn't going back.

He couldn't hold down any job for long. An English teacher (one year), an IELTS coach (four months), a transcriptionist (one year). He was most desirous of travelling alone.

The idea of packing up and defecting from a place, preferably at the stroke of midnight, had always grabbed him. Once, when Shankar was two years old, he wanted to go without mother. His Alfa suitcase was stuffed with a toothbrush, a pack of Gold Flake cigarettes, a Zippo lighter, pants, kurtas, and his ruled composition notebooks filled with his English lessons.

Father stuck mother at his parents' place in Ayikudi, a village in the interiors of South India away from Delhi's cold, until such time he took to figure out his life. Mother offered prayers to Lord Muruga every Sunday in the community temple for her husband to come back to her.

He did come back, a year later—and with fruits. They were mostly prunes. They varied in colour. Orange, red, purple. Bruised ones.

My mother was collecting tulsi leaves in the backyard when my father emerged from practically nowhere and presented her with these prunes. It was magic, witchcraft if you will, but no romance. That night I am guessing, they consummated, as I was born roughly ten months later. The doctors had ruled out a second child, citing my mother's low ovary count, but she had fallen ill with jaundice and typhoid in Ayikudi, which released her eggs. My father was elated and believed that his mystical fruit had a hand in it.

WE FIND WORK IN BANGALORE

Our house in Bangalore was behind the Cantonment Railways Station among the workers' lot. Washerwomen, pan-wallahs, geegaw vendors, and ice-cream concessionaires. Granted, we were not exactly amidst the burghers. My father got the place cheap, Rs 10,000 a month. My mother would wrap some of her halwa in an ever-silver box and offer it to our neighbor's kid. They were poor Tamil Protestants who lived in a shipping container with holes for windows. The patriarch was a drunk and shouted at his wife. They had one married son and a daughter who operated a catering service. They cooked chicken and fish in copper vats which are fired on kilns right outside their doorstep. The daughter-in-law had a four-year-old boy who loved my mother's halwas. They had a dog, a scrawny thing of fur, rescued off the streets. They would tie it to an electricity pole and once it got so shocked that the tip of its tail turned ebony. It hated my father. With my mother, though, it auditioned for a role as her pet. Wagging its tail, making googly eyes at her, doing wheelies on its hind legs.

My decision to become a journalist was as much a matter of choice as it was a timely move. After I matriculated in English, I was twenty-three and looking up the classifieds. One rainy day, my uncle came down from Australia to spend a couple of weeks with us. Uncle was a special sections editor for one of the leading newspapers in Australia. He hadn't forgotten his roots here in the media where he had acquaintances whom he could still call upon for favors.

On that day in Bangalore, he gave me the talk. Father was pottering about in the hall. Uncle told me of a job opportunity in a financial daily. An old friend of his was the editor, he said, and the Bangalore edition was on the search for a copy editor.

"This is your chance, Vishnu. Mumbai is going to see the launch of newspapers and in countries where broadsheets are becoming tabloids and readerships are going down. India is bucking the trend," he said, eyeing my father.

Father was ten years older to Padmanabhan, in a family of four. A father figure. However, the ideals they lived by had put them at a distance. Padma was a conformist. My father often said Padma wanted the safety nets. Meaning: a savings account.

That evening, my father nodded, a touch disappointed that he wasn't giving me the career talk.

"You should take it up, Vishnu. I think it is sound advice coming from someone who is a journalist. In fact," he said, turning to Padma, "I was going to tell Vishnu myself about how the print industry is going through a revival."

"Right. Anyway, here is the number. You can call him and fix up an appointment," my uncle said and scratched out the details of the person on the flipside of his card.

*

The morning of my interview for the financial daily, I took a shower and hurried myself into a blue-collared shirt and black trousers. I found father getting ready to go out, too.

At breakfast, idlis and coconut sambar, he told me he'd finally got a call for a job.

"How about it, Vishnu? One BPO responded," he beamed, swallowing a bite of idli.

B(usiness) P(rocess) O(utsourcing) was the new word of the month whose terms were being defined still. But its effect was already everywhere. College students knew how to roll their 'r's, who the captain of the Boston Red Sox was, and what the weather was like in Seattle.

"What job is it?" I asked.

"Director of communications. Full-time."

Father was wearing a checkered shirt, a tie, drainpipe pants, and lace-up black shoes. His frizzy hair was oiled. He had dyed his sideburns. He finished his idlis, waved to mother, wished me luck, and marched out the door.

After he left, my mother asked me if this was one of his tricks, where he let us think he had a job interview at an MNC, dressed for it but goes instead to the Cubbon Park and wrote his composition notes.

"It is not a hoax," I assured mother.

I vouched for how I had sat with him at that very breakfast table, sending out resumes. I was so certain that father wasn't going anywhere with his career that I regarded the whole endeavor—the shortlisting of job profiles, and the sending of emails—as nothing more than another of his self-delusions.

This time, I was wrong.

THE FLORIDA SHUFFLE

by

JAMES MCADAMS

Author's Note

I started working for Brock Leonard Estredo, aka "Brockenstein," as all the inmates here taunt him, at a GED graduation party he hosted at Turtle Shores Recovery on July 2, 2022, two days before my 30th birthday. We were celebrating our status as high-school equivalency graduates, as well as his recent commendation as a Delray Civic Leader for reducing the cost of overdose cremations through his networking with Lewm Funeral and Memorial World. The estimated savings for 2018-2022 (according to the Delray Coastal Star) was $4 million.

For various reasons involving county budgeting and administrative indifference, The Delray Center for Adult Learners didn't offer a graduation ceremony. Instead, we received our diplomas in the mail along with a sealed ValPak mailer full of coupons for free oil changes, T-Mobile promotions, marijuana dispensary sales, and "Have You Seen Me?" inserts showing pictures of the missing.

Throughout Rehab Alley, these missing-person inserts

could be found mushed in sewage grates and lining litter boxes, or across Meineke counters for free tire rotations. Ghosts. Despite the #1-rated beaches and millionaire time-shares and Spring Break! activities, despite the three All-American Cities awards received (the last in 2017 when thirteen of our high school classmates had died), everyone knew there were two Delrays—one east of the Gulfstream, mansions and yachts merging with West Palm, and one to the west, inhabiting an infernal rhombus drawn by Swinton street, Atlantic avenue, and I-95. This was the epicenter of the opioid epidemic in South Florida. Sometimes, when I awoke from a particularly black binge or batch of laced pills, I'd imagine my own face, scarred and unloved, shrieking at me from the mailer with eyes laced red—"Have You Seen Me?"

Brock owed me because I'd let him cheat off my GED test. I didn't care. The Adult Learners program was a scam just like others. My whole life I'd been surrounded by scams: government scams, family scams, workplace scams, relation-ship scams, court scams, police scams, online dating scams, video game scams, charity scams. Scamming was in the air, the blood, the grids of Delray. Before Brock hired me as a Clean Living Advocate/Resident Advisor at Turtle Shores, I'd never heard of The Florida Shuffle, nor the related crimes of insurance and pharmaceutical fraud I was found guilty of nine months ago. Nor had I set foot in a library since in-school detentions, but now my uniform at Dolphin Correctional Facility (GEO Group) in Delray reads "~~Jimi~~ James McAdams: Librarian."

It's not easy to write this. My hope is that a full account of my experience with The Florida Shuffle will expedite parole. When my best friend Sarah visits, she always says, "You're doing something for others. I hope you're learning about yourself too—and the way I see you."

And it's true, for so long I knew nothing about people, including myself.

Rehab Alley | July 2022

Gage and I were looking for drug zombies to traffic/broker at the NA/AA meeting in the Victims of Opioids Recreation Center in the office plaza on Swinton & 43rd with the AMSCOT and Great Clips. Gage wore a beanie cap and skater jeans. He had business cards with QR codes, fake sobriety chips, and addiction stories stolen from Reddit and Discord. He was another Ashfield survivor and managed Sea of Recovery the way I was about to manage Turtle Shores.

People in town, meaning people on drugs, off drugs, or selling drugs, referred to us as the as the Lost Boys. Vampiric, night-hunters, solemn but insincere, dressed in black. Brock and Gage had been collaborating together for months. They taught me how to be a Zombie Broker. There was a joke going around that Brock was dad and we were his two (adopted) sons.

A girl named Carly, with sharp raven angel hair and an abraded nose she kept touching, was Sharing Her Context with everyone.

"We slept on couches, park benches, a urine-stained recliner on the porch of a hospice in Valdosta, Georgia. Back seats, hatchbacks, haylofts, high-school gyms. We did it for us.

I liked the community. I once slept strapped to the top of the PunkVan, speeding down I-95 towards Richmond, Virginia, waking with a voice like a blender but I killed that gig anyway. We did it for the music and for each other. Bald Goran slept with Neeko, Neeko slept with Miriam, Miriam slept with a teenage fan in Disney World and didn't remember until being informed by Nallie, who slept with the fan's sister, with Bald Goran, with Neeko, with anyone who desired her. I didn't sleep with anyone. I was assaulted, I have walls. And I was sick of the drugs. That's probably why they kicked me out."

The other people, the real people, comforted her. They cooed about vulnerability, self-care, healing, said she had her whole life ahead of her, said she was such a pretty thing. They offered remedies—cold plunges, dopamine fasts, ACE theory, sensory deprivation, veganism, keto, paleo diets. They offered reasons—generational trauma, vitamin B or D deficiency, anemia, pernicious anemia, Lyme disease, gluten and whey allergies. Did she dream and about what? These were their solutions.

When Carly said she'd thought about working at Disney World for the summer to reclaim that feeling of being a child, of every new day being full of possibilities, Gage coughed and raised his hand.

"Everyone who works at Disney World is on the run from something," Gage said. "The law, addiction, spouses, parents, people to whom they've sold cars. They start over in communal dorms, washing lavatories and taxiing rich tourists around the grounds. In the end, the only way they get past it is drug use. I've been there."

Gage had shaved my head and I wore Goodwill clothes not that different than what I normally wore. The combat boots made my ankles sore. I kept applying chapstick to fit in. I texted Brock that we'd found another one. I actually agreed with what she was saying, but there were two choices: 1) suicide or 2) get money and get high. I was good with number two.

By now I'd scavenged enough meetings to decipher some truths: 1) the people with the most advice were the most fucked up; 2) the people who talked the most, always telling their stories, their recovery monologues, were closest to suicide or relapse; 3) coffee was a lousy substitute, with some of them consuming fifteen cups of Folgers a night; 4) they all bit their nails—Carly's actually bleeding; 5) everyone crossed arms across their chest; 6) a bunch of them lamented, and some cried—"I go for walks to town and watch people, and what they do is so easy. Normal is like breathing for them. Why can't I do it? I could never do it. Do you think it's my fault?"; 7) the happiest people were the most desperate. They claimed to know loving ghosts.

Like most zombies, Carly had ADHD and would move from one subject to another with no discernible logic. "Is it weird that I want to die when people compliment me?" she asked. "If someone eulogizes me, let it be someone who knows me, someone who won't take the easy way out and just make an angel out of me and pretend I was the greatest thing that ever existed. My biography must consist of all the lies I've told, all the horrible things I've done, what a fucking shucker I was. I don't know what that word means, but I heard it once in Indiana. Shucker. Those things are as much me as anything else."

There was silence and then everyone applauded. When she smiled, it looked like a grimace.

*

I was taking notes when Brock arrived at the center. These notes were in the form of annotations in the margins around the worksheet Brock had given us for evaluating targets:

Insurance	Y	N	Maybe
Family	Y	N	Maybe
+ Psych Problems	Y	N	Maybe
Gender	M	F	Other
Access→ Money	Y	N	Maybe
Estimated Revenue $$	minus	Estimated Loss $$	

~~Vivi: self-mutilator, Michigan, one month clean, GREAT INSURANCE!!~~

~~Colin: polysubstance: opiates, indica, Valium, Ketamine, ecstasy, Immodium for withdrawal, daughter (8?) hates him. Insurance N/A.~~

Carly: singer in punk band. PA? Chuck Taylors with safety pins instead of laces, NIHIL spelled on the knuckles of her left hand, overdose video on YouTube, 423 views, 00:06:11.

~~Megan: Mother of two, Chron's disease, looking for lost daughter. No insurance coverage so No Go.~~

Brock stood by the Information and Safety tables. Narcan overdose kits, vitamin supplements, CBD-infused green tea, Kratom infusions, QR code-enabled "Are You an Addict?" assessments, magnetized recovery calendars, and Fentanyl testing strips arrayed in stacked towers like Jenga pieces. At the farthest table by the restrooms and water fountains, I watched Brock flick "What You Need to Know About The Florida Shuffle" brochures into a blue recycling bin. Nobody looked at him, his sunglasses oscillating around the room, beaming.

Before the GED instructor made Brock and I study buddies, I'd never heard of Zombie Brokering, Goblin Marketing, Junkie Flunkies, Naltrex Heads, or Narcan Frequent Flyers. Obviously, I'd known there was something wrong with Delray. This was the goldmine of the opioid crisis, Brock explained one night, driving me home from GED class since my license was suspended, pointing at hundreds of sober homes.

Gage let me have Carly. He said she's more my type He'd taught me that it was more efficient to focus on one prospect instead of wandering all over Delray chasing the zombies back to rehabs or their squats on the Gulfstream boats or the tent community under 95. Gage was right, Carly was the kind of girl I always dated—the kind who always died or ran away. So many girls had died on my watch I'd given up, choosing isolation over grief. But they returned in my dreams as ghosts—indifferent, not like the ones in the movies. They didn't care. They asked me to stop bothering them.

Carly wore tight black jeans and a heavy Goodwill sweater, rare in Florida. The sleeves hid her hands, signs of self-mutilation. Her bangs were self-cut and hung like a waterfall over the left side of her face. The Hello Kitty bag next to her chair had a chain attached and little slogans written in black Sharpie: "Everyone's A Hypocrite"; "LOVE is just a 4-Letter word." Her posture, coiled up in the chair with her arms around her knees, making herself as small as possible, suggested a history of sexual abuse and intimacy issues. Brock taught me that.

The back entrance to the Rec Center was separated by a parking lot from a lake polluted from refuse thrown off I-95 and the PHOA runoff. There were dead fish and duck corpses floating between leaves from withered trees. I found Carly looking over the pond of death with her arms crossed, elbows in her hands, distant from the rest of the group wishing each other the best of luck and trading numbers for prayer chains and emergency contacts.

"Was your rabbit really at your intervention?" I asked, referencing one of her mumbled, sarcastic comments at the meeting.

According to Brock, we should blame the PHOA thing for the lack of reproduction in West Palm County. Carly turned to me. "Why are all the fish dead?" She looked even smaller and more vulnerable standing than fetal in her chair.

"You're not from around here?" I guessed. "It just happens. Algae blooms."

"*Here* being where fish die?"

"There's a lot of toxins. Again, it just happens down here."

"Red Tide?"

"You could call it that and not be that wrong."

"So you live here and don't care?"

Her cigarette had no filter. I could tell she was looking for someplace to throw the butt.

"You can just toss it. The pond's already dead. Everything's dead."

"It's all good." She extinguished the butt with her tongue and tucked it back into the pack. She walked away from the pond. I followed her back up to the parking lot. She stopped and leaned against a truck, six feet away from me. "Sarah told me to watch for you."

"Me? You don't know me."

"People, like you. Body brokers, recruiters. How much can you make off me?"

There were sliding scales, I could have told her. As much as $10,000 a month and as little as $500 a month. That was just my takeaway. Once, when Brock was giving me a ride home, he'd taken a call, talking mostly in code, but before hanging up he'd said, "nothing less than half a mil." Gage had bought two condos and three cars in the last year. The money was massive, untaxed, unsupervised, flowing from Delray to Boca Raton and even as far away as Ocala and the University of South Florida body farm in Pasco County, where the fentanyl and xylazine corpses were sold for the grad students to experiment on.

"You should bring your rabbit down from Philly. It'll help. My cat helped me get better. Do you have a pic?"

"Places don't allow it. They want to strip us of everything, of all meaning and context, and once we're isolated like that, they can help. Or what they call help."

There's a picture of us in the parking lot outside the Rec Center that I still have in my prison cell. Brock took it. Carly leaning against the truck and me looking too tall, too skinny, too jittery, barefooted in cargo shorts. Sarah won't look at the picture anymore. She says everything that happened after was obvious. I was a predator. But at that time I really felt that I wasn't a bad person, I was just trying to get money. That's what we're all doing, right? Money is value. Value is pleasure. We all want pleasure. Does it matter how you get it? Love, crime, drugs, fraud, kids, pets, travel, charity, food, clean sheets.

"I'm just saying, this place helped me, it's right over there. Sea of Recovery. They allow pets. My cat's better now too. Do what you want. Doesn't matter to me."

"I'm supposed to meet my friend Sarah at another place. We met at a rehab in Boca."

"This place is better, believe me. She'll end up there anyway. How many places could there be?"

She'd never guess the correct answer was over a hundred.

"Let me guess. You can pull strings to get me in there? You can get me a discount? And you're doing this all as Mr. Charity?"

"Exactly," I said. "You came to a support meeting and I'm giving you support. What could be in it for me?"

"What's the worst that could happen?" she asked. She was trying to joke but she looked down and grimaced. I remembered that question for a long time.

"My friend runs it. I could get him to sneak in your rabbit for you. I'm a nice guy."

"Famous last words," she said, but she came towards me and took a business card.

Thirty minutes later, she trudged away with my directions to Sea of Recovery. She'd been out of rehab one week and had unlimited insurance through her parents. She'd shown me her overdose video as a goof, but I think she was just lonely and needed to talk. I've seen enough of them to know they are the most intimate records, more intimate than a sex video for sure. The overdose video meant the sober home manager could blackmail her if she tried to leave, threatening to send it to her family, colleagues, bosses, nieces, nephews, and anyone else in her harried radius. She was a AAA candidate for which I would receive $500 upon admission and $1,000 for each completed month of her stay, all via crypto wallet.

When she left, Brock ambled up next to me, holding his flip-flops because the water by the pond's edge was dewy with chemical runoff, condoms, syringes, and candy bags. He flexed his tanned biceps as he ran them through his sparkly gelled buzzcut.

"Another one," I said, nodding towards Carly.

"You'll be Zombie Broker of the week third time in a row," Brock said. "Deserves a bonus."

"How much will she be worth?"

He shrugged, grabbing his money clip and removing hundreds. "Five thousand a month. Give or take."

"And it's all the urine tests?"

"Liquid gold, my friend. Physical therapy, occupational therapy, anything can be billed."

"So why do I only get $1,000?"

He stopped counting. I watched Carly recede up the street, just another girl walking down the dangerous streets of Delray. When she reached Sea of Recovery, she looked back at me like, "Is this the one?"

I nodded and pointed like, "Go, Go!"

She started up the path, then stopped and waved. It was a halting wave, she was trying to come across as careless, but she was scared. I wondered if she was even twenty-one.

"Told you before, we assume all the risk," Brock said. "You talked to a cute girl, even got a cigarette and her number, and for that you get $1,500 right now."

"I'm risking stuff too."

"We're ahead of the law. What you just did, Jimi, is legal and American."

"And what you do?"

He winked at me. "That's the real America."

I pocketed Brock's cash and reclined in the wet spiky grass, sighing. I felt like a python that wouldn't have to eat for two months.

"About your promotion…"

"What promotion?"

"Tell you more at the GED party."

"There's no ceremony, they don't give a shit about us."

"My party, my man. The recovery place at Turtle Shores, I don't want a bunch of strangers in my *casa*, you understand." He leaned into me and shushed. He was the kind of person who laughed loudly at his own jokes.

"I have an opening for a full-time job at Turtle Shores if you want it," he added. "That's the promotion."

"What should I bring?"

Brock crumpled his face to show he was thinking. "Bring your life, everything you'll miss. A room will be ready for you." He gestured at my clothes. "It's time for Jimi 2.0, don't you agree?"

It wasn't the first time Brock had intuited, somehow, what

a waste my life was. He reminded me of an FBI profiler, or an "empath," the kind of person who can read you in a second. Sometimes people like that become sociopaths, of course, but in his case, it made sense that he'd become a successful businessman and community official. At that time, he owned Sea of Recovery and Turtle Shores along with three sober houses, two car washes, and a float therapy clinic, whereas everything I owned was stuffed into Amazon boxes in my uncle's guest room closet at Swan's Grove 55+ Retirement Community.

For most of my twenties, I slept on couches in basements or unfurnished guest rooms all day, drank and snorted benzos and opiates every night. I'd never graduated high school, held a salaried job, had a checking account, signed a rental lease, or dated a girl for more than two months. I couldn't iron a shirt, tie a tie, put oil in an engine, correctly place out the forks and knives, or even trim my nails. My jobs were random and temporary: Fiverr Sockpocket, CBD brewery barback, Grub-hub driver, webcam videographer, online dating profile writer, software tester, telemarketer.

I'd begun to figure my life was just what it was, not a thing I controlled but a sort of hideous emanation without source.

"I'm ready for a new me," I joked to Brock, hinting at a famous recovery pledge.

He explained I would assume the role of a Clean Living Advocate at Turtle Shore Recovery for $500/week plus room and board. My room was in a renovated shed that looked out on Ashfield Memorial Park, where I threw a no-hitter in elementary school, and the overflowing cemetery behind it, where my high school class had buried over fifty students since 2006 due to overdose, suicide, or incidents in Iraq/Afghanistan.

"You'll dispense medications, drive the transport vehicle, assist the residents in activities of daily living, join in on therapy sessions by the pool, type up progress notes on a HIPAA-protected server," he said. "Keep your head down and mouth shut. Don't tell me you have anything better to do."

"Only one problem... I have a DUI," I said, "I can't drive."

Brock waved his hand. "I know a judge. So, Turtle Shores off Swinton and Atlantic. Can't miss it."

"How legit is the job?"

"Like you care if things are legit." He snorted. "You always need to know everything. Just come to the party and have some fun, man. The rest will happen as God wants."

"That's what I'm afraid of," I mumbled. By the time we left, the lights were off on the Sea of Recovery lawn and Carly was nowhere to be seen. I pulled out the cassette she'd given me when I said I knew people in the music business. "READY FOR THE NEW ME," she'd written on the label.

COOLER HEADS

by

JULIAN TEPPER

5

DOWN SOUTH

Celia was eager to get down to Knoxville to see her family before she was too pregnant to fly. Though her mother and stepfather had moved away, first to Hawaii and then Indiana to pursue better-paying jobs, Celia's father and his wife were still living in her hometown. The relative ease of the first trimester had given way to more months of good health. If you asked Celia how she was feeling, she would tell you she was absolutely fine.

It was the first question put to her by her father, D.W. He had arrived at the Knoxville airport thirty minutes late to pick us up, unsurprisingly, as it were. Like his accent, his life had a kind of drawl to it, a lag. His height seemed to have something to do with this. It took effort to lift those large feet and extend his long legs and carry forward his upper bulk. You wouldn't tell a giant to hurry up for the obvious reason that he might use his strength on you, but also because he wouldn't be able to go any faster if he tried. D.W. called his daughter Nippers, as in, "How was the flight, Nippers?" and spoke with a gentleness that could almost be mistaken for sadness. He carried his daughter's suitcase, despite the handle and wheels available to him, lumbering through the uncrowded baggage claim, a bit off-kilter and about six feet ahead of us.

He was silent in the white Jeep Cherokee, riding back to the house. Celia tried to make small talk: she inquired about Lily, D.W.'s wife of some ten years, tried to find out how her school year was going—she taught fourth grade—and the latest on Lily's sons. D.W. answered, though never with more than three words. I sat in the back of the car not saying much myself. I had already met D.W. and Lily during a trip to Knoxville some eight months back. If our past visit had told me anything, it was that D.W. was open-minded and could accept that his then married daughter was in an open relationship and seeing other people. That is, in his quiet style, he had treated me with kindness and decency. I also learned that he would offer me a very tall glass of whiskey and ice the moment we came in the door and that he would keep my glass full for the remainder of the trip, and for that I was grateful.

But then shortly after arriving at his home, with Celia and I having put our suitcases down and said hello to Lily and settled onto the patio overlooking the bean-shaped swimming pool, D.W. handed me a glass of tepid water with a single ice cube and then lowered himself onto a folding chair that nearly collapsed beneath his weight. Taking a moment to find his voice, he finally said, "Listen here, son—you listening?—you are going to marry my Celia, all right? You hearing me?"

I didn't doubt that I had heard him correctly. The severity of his tone assured me that I had understood him, too. Celia sat silently in a chair near the pool's edge, her big brown eyes downcast and her painter's hands folded on the curvature of her stomach. Lily, a redheaded daughter of Knoxville, a tall, ex-beauty contestant, set a tray of salty snacks down onto a picnic table and said, "Now, D.W., please," but nothing more.

In the folding chair beside D.W., I took in a mouthful of the lukewarm water, holding it at the back of my throat before swallowing. "Sir," I said, "I appreciate where you're coming from—"

"What? You appreciate it, son?"

"Yes, but I don't know if Celia and I will get married. I'm sorry, but—"

"Oh, no, no—you're not hearing me, Paul. You are not hearing me."

"And, right, yes, well, I mean, Celia and I have discussed marrying and I just can't say with any confidence that it's where she and I are heading and—"

"Young man, you are not hearing me."

"Yes, I know, but here's the thing, sir, because I want to spend my whole life with your daughter and I want to be buried in the plot directly next to hers and I know that one hundred and ten percent, and you have my word and I'd write it for you in blood."

"Paul! Do you have a hearing problem? Answer me. Do you? Can you not hear, son?"

"No, sir. I do not have a hearing problem."

"Are you sure? Have you had your hearing checked? Have you? Have you been to a doctor?"

"I have not, sir."

"Well, you might want to schedule an appointment."

D.W.'s gaze was set forward toward the cool clear sky above. Exhaling, tense and laboring, he said, "Now if I have to drag your ass to the chapel, son, I will drag your ass to the chapel."

"Sir, I don't—"

"Son, I will put you in that flippin' car out front and I will haul your ass up the drive and down the road to that chapel. Do you hear me?"

"Yes, sir. I think I do, but—"

"Because you are marrying my daughter."

"Okay. Thank you, yes."

"You are marrying her."

"Yep. Yes. Yes, I am."

D.W. stood, his giant mass unfolding part by part until it assumed a towering presence over me. His right eye twitched, his dimpled chin held drops of sweat. I didn't know if he would pick me up next and throw me into the swimming pool, where an orange Volunteers raft floated on the surface of the water. D.W. himself seemed unsure what to do now, his body perhaps in conflict with itself, as if his head and limbs could not agree on a direction. I braced, then I heard D.W. huff and all of a sudden he was marching back into the house.

Lily flashed us a concerned look and then followed after him.

Once the sliding glass door had closed behind her, I rose from my seat, and said, "Holy fucking hell."

"You did great, baby."

"Great? You think so?"

"He loves me so much. Can you blame him? It really was

very sweet of him."

"I mean, sure, okay, but is he going to fucking kill me?"

"Daddy? No."

The color in Celia's cheeks was full, ruddy. Her eyes gleamed with pride.

I lowered to my knees, taking her hands. I said, "You know I do want to spend my whole life with you and be buried next to you? You know that, don't you? I meant that."

"You promise?"

"Absolutely—yes, I promise."

"Should we get married then?"

"I don't know. Maybe we should," I said, kissing Celia's pregnant stomach. "We could."

"I just don't know what I think of marriage anymore."

"I understand. But maybe our kid will be happier if his parents are married."

"That could be."

"Maybe we do get married. Maybe I'm going to put a large rock on your finger."

"You will not."

"Maybe I will—a big rock for the whole village to see."

"You better not," said Celia, squeezing me close to her. "Just tell me you love me and that you always will."

"I love you and I always will," I said.

"You promise me, Paul?"

"I do. I promise, I promise," I said. "Now let's go find a hotel."

6
NURSERY RHYMES

Graham had moved nearby into an old warehouse on Driggs in Williamsburg, a sprawling industrial space that he shared with friends. Offered a bedroom there, he had opted for a large closet. He slept on a wooden plank and used a two-by-four in place of a pillow. In Graham's estimation, denying himself these basic comforts was a nod to the order of the monks whom he so greatly admired. Was he upset about his wife leaving him? How about her carrying another man's child? He had never said anything about it directly to Celia, nor had he addressed me on the matter. But after moving out of the apartment, he had ridden a bicycle from New York to Seattle, sleeping in ditches along the side of the road. On the journey, he lost nearly a third of his already negligible body weight. He had briefly planned to move to Micronesia, an island located somewhere between Hawaii and the Philippines, which sounded both made up and like a cry for help. His relocation had been contingent on a job offer, one that had ultimately been rescinded, and so instead of being employed on a remote island on the other side of the world he was now working for a woodworker right here in Brooklyn.

He had promised Celia that he would do some work around the apartment before our child was born, attend to some of the long-standing problems that predated my arrival: the broken lock on the bathroom window, a doorknob that had continued to fall off, a shim-job on an off-balanced bookcase, a leak under the kitchen sink, a lamp that had to be rewired, a chair leg that needed reinforcement. Celia and I left the apartment for a couple of hours so that he could come over and do the work one Saturday shortly before her due date and when we returned what we discovered was not only a fixed bathroom window and a new doorknob and a shimmed bookcase, but an entire nursery custom-built by Graham.

"This is fucking insane," I said.

"I know, look at the crib, it's fit for a prince," said Celia, holding the hump of her stomach in the crook of her arm.

The crib was exquisite, made of a cocoa-colored wood. Next to the crib were cubbies, twelve squares, four across and three levels high, a handsome piece of furniture on which Graham had placed a brand-new light-up globe. There was a changing table with a built-in drawer, its knob inlaid with mother-of-pearl. Who knew how many hours of work he had put into building these pieces—ten, fifteen, maybe twenty or more? Celia and I drew our hands up and down the furniture in a state of utter disbelief. Graham had said nothing to prepare us for this, not a word. There was a card in which Graham explained how excited he was for the birth of our child and how this nursey was an expression of those feelings.

"Do you think we should say something, Celia?"

"Like what?"

"Like: seek help."

"That's not funny, Paul."

"I agree. None of this is funny."

"Come on, he's done such great work. Who could argue with that?"

"I could. I could argue with all of it."

"But you won't. Now stop, please."

Celia insisted on having Graham over the following night so that we could toast to his efforts with a few rounds of Fernet, his favorite spirit. Graham arrived wearing the Sherlock Holmes hat and carrying a pipe he didn't smoke but merely held while he went on for more than forty minutes about the inspiration for the nursery: the furniture in a monastery that he and Celia had visited in Tuscany in their early twenties. We hadn't even gotten to the Fernet nor the hors d'oeuvres Celia had picked up earlier in the day. I was about to propose we do so, but then Graham took some kind of butter cookie out of the pocket of his suit jacket and began nibbling on it. Crumbs fell on his collar and on the floor. He spoke with his mouth full.

"I'm so sorry, Paul," he said, interrupting himself mid-thought. "I've been talking the whole time, haven't I?"

Celia glared at me, arms crossed.

I held up my hands, shook my head. "No, no, carry on. I'm interested in all of it."

"You're sure?" said Graham.

"Absolutely."

Graham smiled. Then he began to describe how monks in medieval times would have kept their prayer books on a piece of furniture that almost exactly resembled the new changing table, then about how he had driven to a special lumber yard four hours away in Pennsylvania where a particular strain of mahogany could be had and not for cheap, and then there was at least another half hour of Graham talking about the two all-nighters he had pulled so that he could sneak into a friend's workshop in the off-hours and use its high-end machinery (saws, sanders). I sat there, drinking steadily, though I did not like Fernet, and at some point it occurred to me that I was very drunk and also that this apartment was bursting with Graham's furniture and that it couldn't hold any more of it and that I had to push back.

"Excuse me a moment, everyone."

Celia and Graham didn't seem to notice me stand and go into the bedroom. In the corner was the chest built by Graham, which I emptied onto the floor—socks, underwear, sweatpants, T-shirts. The chest was ever-slightly larger than I imagined, cumbersome in my arms and pinching at the skin. On seeing me enter the kitchen now, Graham and Celia both rose from their seats.

"Graham," I said, "I'm putting this at the door. Take it with you tonight when you leave."

"Oh, no, no," said Graham, holding the pipe out toward me, his brow creased under the brim of the Sherlock hat. "That's yours, Paul."

"No, no, no, no, it's yours. You're taking it."

"He wants you to have it," said Celia. She'd tied back her hair tonight with a red ribbon, her unobstructed eyes big, clear, purposeful.

I placed the chest at the door. "It's a great piece, Graham. Gorgeous, truly. You do such good work. But take it with you tonight. I have a new chest coming."

"You ordered a new chest?" said Celia.

"No, not yet. But soon, tomorrow. Graham, you'll take the chest. It's your chest. Take the chest."

"Paul, I want you to have that chest."

"No. It's yours. Take it with you, please, for the love of God!"

We stood in silence around the untouched hors d'oeuvres. I could feel Celia staring at me, the intensity of her look. Heat moved through my cheeks, my arms and hands, down to my feet.

"It's a great chest, Graham, but I don't want it. Take it with you tonight. Okay?"

"Okay," said Graham.

"Thank you."

Graham put his hand on my shoulder now, leaning in close to me. "If you want, Paul…if you don't like the chest, I could make you a new one. Would that be better? I'm happy to make one for you if you like. It wouldn't be a problem. No, it would be my pleasure. I mean it."

7
BLIZZARDS & BIRTHS

Celia's contractions began during a blizzard on the night of December 28. In good weather the Natural Birthing Center in Upper Manhattan was a thirty-minute car ride from our apartment, but there was almost two feet of snow accumulated on the ground and who knew how our taxi driver would even navigate his car in these conditions. The black sedan was parked outside the apartment. The time was 4:02 a.m. Visibility was almost none. The traffic lights were all being tossed about like buoys in choppy water. Garbage bags tied to receptacles on street corners were turned inside out by the wind and blowing around as if lifted by angry spirits. In the backseat of the car, Celia's contractions were slowing down, and by the time we arrived at the birthing center they had stopped completely.

Inside, Celia and I were sent into a small room with a queen-sized bed and a standing lamp. What about Celia's contractions? The midwives explained that in the process of traveling from home they had receded, which was normal, we would simply have to wait for them to start up again. How long that would take was anyone's guess, but Celia and I were just so grateful to have made it here in the blizzard. One of the midwives said we ought to be, that a mother scheduled to deliver at the birthing center had been unable to get out of her apartment building, the front door barricaded by snow, and she had given birth at home in her apartment as the midwives had talked her husband through the steps of how to support her.

We were told to make ourselves comfortable. But just then, Celia cried out in pain. Her contractions were back. The next one came in less than three minutes. Celia was breathing heavily, her hands on the bulk of her stomach as if to slow the pressure caused by the oncoming baby. The contractions that followed were less than two minutes apart.

"This is the worst pain of my life. God, it hurts."

I went to find the midwives. Perhaps owing to my exhaustion or stress or both, I could hardly tell the four of them apart. Between forty and fifty years old, about five foot four inches tall, one hundred and ten pounds, blonde to strawberry-blonde hair, gaunt, pale, wiry, and in motion—no, they didn't stop moving from point to point to point around the birthing center, tending to responsibilities. One midwife in training was easy to tell apart because she had none of the skill or deliberateness of the other midwives. Her name was Lucy. She was glad to hear the contractions had intensified. She would check the heart rate of the baby. To do so, she would have to locate the whereabouts of the baby's heart with a fetal monitor. Lucy, light bleary eyes, tangled reddish-blonde hair, tentative, drew the device over Celia's pelvic area, searched and searched but found nothing.

"Sorry," said Lucy. "It's really hard to find the heartbeat. Don't worry. I'm not worried. It's there. I'll get it."

I was prepared to tear the fetal monitor out of Lucy's hand and pinpoint the heartbeat myself. Instead, Merry, the midwife who seemed to do everything around here—file the paperwork, answer the phones, vacuum the carpets, examine the expecting mothers and deliver their babies—came into the room and did it.

"There it is," said Merry, the transducer held directly beneath Celia's belly button. The heart rate was steady, strong. The thumping of the baby's heart was the most glorious sound. Merry, who wore a red bandana over her head of long blonde hair and a pencil behind her ear, said: "How do you feel, Celia? Are you comfortable? You need anything?"

"No, I'm fine," said Celia.

But at the next moment, Celia's labor began to rapidly accelerate. Now Merry and Lucy were on either side of her, with two additional midwives present, and were telling Celia not to push yet. They would say when. Not yet, no. Wait. Wait. Now.

"Push!" they told Celia.

Celia, seated at a slight angle on the bed, knees up, legs open, gown hoisted just past her buttocks, pushed with all her might, teeth clenched, eyes tightly shut, face bright red. One, two, three, push. One, two, three, push. Celia let out a deep moan—and then the midwives instructed her to stop pushing. She had to wait. They would let her know when she could start pushing again. And now here it came, and they told her to push, with Celia engaging what appeared to be every muscle in her body from her toes up through her forehead. Merry was seated between Celia's splayed legs and she said she could see the baby's head. Could she? The head? Could it be that this would all be over soon, the baby born, and Celia holding our child in her arms?

Merry instructed Celia to keep doing exactly what she was doing and to not change a thing. Her gaze was steady. "You've got this, Celia. You're almost done."

"You're there," said Lucy, hovering at the foot of the bed.

The two additional midwives who had come into the room were rooting Celia on, clapping, applauding. "You're a superstar, Celia. You've got this."

"You're doing it, Celia. You're getting there."

"Celia," said Merry, "just a little bit more. Just a little bit more."

But the baby's head, though crowning, was proving too large to exit Celia. Perhaps the midwives could help her find a better angle at which to push the baby out. Merry proposed drawing Celia a bath—there was a large tub in the bathroom—and she could stand up in the hot water and gravity would do something to assist in the process and Celia would be able to engage different muscles and push even harder. Celia agreed. It sounded promising. It looked so, too. Celia, stooped in the bath, her feet a good distance apart, left hand holding onto a metal bar, appeared primed to birth the baby. Merry asked her to push and Celia gave it her all, moaning deeply.

"Push! Push, Celia!" said Merry.

"Come on, Celia. You can do it. Push!" cried Lucy, as did the other midwives.

But with the next push, still nothing.

Celia flashed a dispirited look, one that brought a somberness to all the midwives.

"The baby's not coming out," she said. "I think his head is too large to get through. I've never been in so much pain in my life. Should we go to the hospital?"

"No. Not yet," said Merry. "Let's get you back in the bed, Celia, take vitals, and do a little more pushing. If you can have the baby here, that'll be for the best. Let's just give it one more try."

"I don't know how much more I can do," said Celia.

"Okay," said Merry. "I know. I know. Birthing a child is serious work. You've got this, though. You can do this."

A minute later, Celia was in the bed, and Merry, checking the baby's heart rate, noted that it had become slower.

Celia seemed to gather all her strength, repositioning herself at a slight angle. Her hands clutched the sheets, her toes curled. The midwives were urging her on, as was I, seated directly behind her. Merry said that she would count to three and then Celia should push. Here it came, this was it, the child would be born here and now, yes.

"Ready, Celia? Okay, here we go," said Merry. Her tone was stern. This was an order to push out her baby. "One, two, three!"

Celia began to push with her whole being. She released

a sound that was part war cry, part plea for mercy. The baby's head was touchable, ready to emerge. And yet the head could not fit through, and there was nothing Celia could do now to change this fact. No amount of pushing would help.

An ambulance was called. The nearest hospital, Columbia Presbyterian, was about fifteen blocks away, but the streets were snow locked. The 911 dispatch wasn't willing to promise that an ambulance would even be able to make it to the address of the birthing center.

"Is an ambulance coming or not?" I asked Merry.

"Yes, yes, an ambulance is coming...I think."

"We'll get you to the hospital," I told Celia. "Don't worry. Let's get you dressed."

"I can't put on pants," she said. The baby was fully descended, the head partially out, the pressure immense. "Everything inside me wants to keep pushing."

"Hold on, you will get to push so soon," I said. "We'll be at that hospital in no time and you'll get to push and then you'll be holding our baby."

"Pass me my coat. I'm just going to wrap myself in it. Then let's go wait outside." So many blood vessels in her eyes had burst. I wrapped Celia in her coat.

In the vestibule of the birthing center, Celia and I held hands, quiet, numb, waiting. Minutes passed, beneath the low light of a single bulb. How was the baby doing? What was its heart rate? Was it still alive? Would the ambulance make it here? And if not, would we carry Celia through the blizzard for nearly a mile? Perhaps that's just how it would have to happen. Maybe we would hitch a ride from one of the trucks plowing the streets.

An ambulance pulled up in front of the birthing center. Two EMTs emerged, one with a clipboard, one with a gurney. Celia, coat draped over her shoulders, in sweater and boots but no pants, lay down on the gurney. Merry, Lucy, and the two other midwives, out in the wind and snow, told her not to worry, she would be fine. She had done an incredible job. The baby would soon be out, they promised.

I hurried alongside the gurney, as the EMTs wheeled Celia into the back of the ambulance. When the doors slammed, Celia and I looked at one another, a long silent exchange that required no words at all. The ambulance pulled out, and we were on our way to the hospital. Celia and I held hands, feeling the road beneath the tires, this icy passage. Through two small windows at the back of the ambulance, I saw abandoned cars littered throughout the streets in deep snow. The wind outside sounded monstrous, as if it could tear off a side of the vehicle.

"We're two blocks from the hospital, Celia. We're about to get that baby into your arms."

"I know we are," she said.

"Good. Just hold on, just hold on."

The ambulance pulled up at the emergency room entrance and within seconds the EMTs had the gurney out and were wheeling Celia into the ER. There was no signing in, just a straight passage through the bright fluorescent-lit hospital corridor into an elevator up to a higher floor, and at last, into an operating room.

A man walked in, brown mustache, blue scrubs, white latex gloves, medical mask hung around his neck, and he introduced himself as Dr. Mark. He no doubt recognized the look of trauma on Celia's face. Three nurses moved efficiently about the room, following the doctor's orders. The device in Dr. Mark's hand was called a vacuum but resembled a toilet plunger. Next thing, Dr. Mark brought the vacuum between Celia's legs and applied the suction cup to the end of the baby's crowning head.

"Okay, Celia, I'm going to count to three and then say push. Okay?"

"Yes," she said, two hands clutching the railings of the operating table.

"One...two...three...push!"

Celia let out a scream, and the doctor proceeded to pull on the vacuum with what looked to me like all his strength. Then suddenly, the suction cup popped off the baby's head.

Pop!

I was sure our child was dead. Vitals of both mother and baby were taken. Celia, who was not on any pain drugs, did not even make a sound. Her eyes looked out straight ahead at the doctor, who was now applying the vacuum to the baby's head a second time.

"All right, Celia...one, two, three, okay?"

"Yes, yes. Okay."

Again, Celia cried out, and Dr. Mark pulled hard on the vacuum, and again:

Pop!

Silence from Celia, the nurses, too.

"Okay, so here's the story," said Dr. Mark, poised, calm. "I'm going to put this vacuum on your baby's head once again and you're going to push him out, and if it doesn't work, we'll have to do a C-section."

"Just get the baby out of me!" said Celia. "Do whatever you have to do! Please!"

I pressed my hand to Celia's shoulder. Vitals were taken again. The baby's heart rate was lowering. Same with Celia's. Dr. Mark brought the suction cup to the baby's head a third time.

"All right, Celia, I want you to push with all you've got. Give it one really, really hard push, and we'll get the baby out of you right now. Okay? You're going to do it. You'll do it right now. You're ready? Good, good. I know you're ready! On three."

"Okay," she said.

"One...two...three!"

And Celia began to scream and push, and Dr. Mark was pulling so hard on the vacuum, and suddenly—suddenly—there was a baby in Dr. Mark's hands, and he cried out:

"It's a healthy baby boy!"

Dr. Mark placed the wailing baby on Celia's breast.

At the sight of Celia and the newborn, I began to weep. "Look at him," I said to Celia. "Look at that baby."

"Oh my God, my baby," she said, breathless, panting. "My baby, my baby, it's my baby."

"Celia, Celia, look at that baby. Our baby. Dr. Mark, did you see that!"

"I did. I saw it. Congratulations to you both," he said. "You make a beautiful family."

"Oh, my baby," said Celia, stroking the nursing newborn's red, swollen face. Tears streamed from her eyes. She said, "Paul, my love, come here, come close, come all the way in."

I brought my cheek to her cheek. "Celia, my love, you did it, you did it, you did it."

"We did it," she whispered into my ear. "We're a family now."

<u>EXCERPT</u> Magazine No. 2

CONTRIBUTORS

Mara Aguilar Egan is a fictionist and poet residing in the mountains of Western North Carolina. She received the Sullivan Writing Scholar award for excellence in both playwriting and fiction and her MFA from Queens University of Charlotte where she served as head fiction editor of Qu Magazine. Her work has been supported by Bread Loaf Environmental Writers Conference and Tin House Workshop. Her Pushcart Prize and Best of Net nominated stories have appeared in Vestal Review, SmokeLong Quarterly, Litbreak Magazine, and others. Her current writing fixates on ecosystem, on what it means to belong to a land, to a history, and to one another when the world we were promised is not what we've inherited.

Synopsis: A decade after swearing to never return to his hometown in Southern Appalachia, Dennis does just that. He has given himself one week to make amends with his ailing mother, his brother, and the unrealized love he left behind, in the hopes he'll finally be free of the past for good. But when he finds himself stranded at his former, now derelict, summer camp, Dennis begins to unearth both real and imagined ghosts from his past: an old obsession with the camp's haunted lore, his own mother's hidden history, and the mystery of his best friend's death on the campgrounds ten years ago. When everything he thought he knew falls apart, Dennis must choose once again whether to stay or go, and learn what it means to belong when all we have inherited is on fire.

*

CONTRIBUTORS

Chrissy Kolaya is a poet and fiction writer, author of *Charmed Particles: a novel* (Dzanc Books 2015) and two books of poems: *Any Anxious Body* and *Other Possible Lives* (Broadstone Books 2014, 2019). Her work has been included in anthologies by Norton, Milkweed Editions, and a number of literary journals. You can learn more at chrissykolaya.com

Synopsis: *The Second Voyage of Audley Worthington* tells tells the story of a 19th Century naturalist who mysteriously disappears while searching Clove Island for what he suspects may be—in the scientific parlance of the time—a missing link between humans and apes. When Worthington returns to the island in hopes of traveling deep into the interior, he must reckon with the consequences of his first expedition and the island's subsequent colonization, while his indigenous guide Tanok must decide whether to accompany Worthington on his trip in search of a small human-like creature known as the yu-mau. A century later, fossil remains discovered on Clove Island raise questions about the indigenous stories of the yu-mau—long discounted by Westerners as nothing more than folktales.

*

Alex Kuzio is a writer, instructor, and higher education administrator. He earned his MFA in Creative Writing from Queens University of Charlotte, where he served as a fiction editor of Qu Magazine and a contributing writer to The Southern Review of Books. He lives in Philadelphia with his wife and son. *Orphans* is his first novel and he's working on a second one.

Synopsis for *Orphans*: In the woods outside Tallahassee, a religious cult, holed up in a compound, is raided by the FBI.

EXCERPT Magazine No. 2

In the ensuing firefight, all the adult members are killed, leaving a bunker full of orphaned children with nowhere left to go. As two of the rescued children—teenaged Eunice and her little brother Zachary—wait in a motel room to learn their fate, Eunice reflects back on the loss and terror—and occasional beauty—of growing up in the compound, and searches for new meaning in the strange world outside its thick walls. Meanwhile, in a Pennsylvania college town, Sally and Adam—their marriage floundering after they learn they cannot have children—react in horror to reports of the cult's shocking rituals of violence. As these four lives barrel toward one another, America itself struggles to agree on what actually happened in Tallahassee, as wild conspiracy theories challenge the official explanation.

*

Cora Lewis is a writer and reporter whose fiction has appeared at The Yale Review, Joyland, Epiphany, Juked, GASHER Journal, and elsewhere. Her nonfiction has appeared in The Wall Street Journal, New York Observer, and BuzzFeed News. She received her MFA from Washington University in St. Louis and her BA from Yale University. She currently works at the Associated Press in New York.

Synopsis: *The Information Age*, a novel from life told in vignettes, follows a journalist at an online news site as she comes of age in New York during a time of information overload. Drawing on dialogue from professional and personal encounters, emails, texts, and message board comments, the protagonist works to make sense of news real and fake, campaign trail rhetoric, dating app exchanges, the rise of Artificial Intelligence, and other perils and pleasures of a life lived at the internet's pace.

CONTRIBUTORS

Karthik Krishnan's fiction has appeared or is forthcoming in Fiction on the Web, The Chakkar, and The Usawa Literary Review. He lives with his wife and kids in Hyderabad, India.

Synopsis: *My Father's Toolkit* is a serio-comic novel that explores the dynamic between a father and a son in the early years of the new century. It takes on the call centre culture, financial markets, and what it means to lead a middle-class life divorced from its notions of money and class.

*

James McAdams teaches full-time in Purdue Global's English and Rhetoric Department and adjuncts at the University of South Florida and Ringling College of Art + Design. James McAdams' debut short story collection, Ambushing the Void, was published by Frayed Edge Press (May 2020). Formerly Flash Fiction Editor at Barren Magazine, he received his Ph.D. in English Literature from Lehigh University. His work can be viewed at www.jamesmcadams.org.

Synopsis for *The Florida Shuffle*: In Delray—the epicenter of the opioid crisis in South Florida—thousands have died of overdose, suicide, or substance-abuse related conditions. Meanwhile, James McAdams makes his living exploiting addicts in sober homes via urinalysis tests, sex trafficking, and lab kickbacks. He lives reckless and heedless, chasing pleasure alone, until his ex-girlfriend Sarah arrives at the sober home he manages. After multiple clients overdose and he's imprisoned for fraud, Sarah encourages James to write about "The Florida Shuffle" as a path to redemption. Read, learn, protect, forgive. Remember our ghosts.

EXCERPT Magazine No. 2

Julian Tepper is the author of the novels Between the Records, Balls, Ark, and Cooler Heads. His writing has appeared in the Paris Review, Playboy, The Brooklyn Rail, Zyzzyva, The Daily Beast, Tablet Magazine, and elsewhere. He was born and raised in New York City and lives there still.

Synopsis: *Cooler Heads* (Rare Bird 2024) is a novel about modern love. With a triangulation of lovers and spouses, young children and struggling careers, Celia and Paul are two people in that pocket of life when the fight to figure out who we are and what we want burns brightest. Their story is a meditation on the limits of what we can and cannot have, set in a city—New York—that would have us think that we can have it all. *Cooler Heads* is available now through Rare Bird Books.

{ FIN }

www.ingramcontent.com/pod-product-compliance
Lightning Source LLC
Chambersburg PA
CBHW051304250626
47155CB00009B/3430